The Lady Grace Mysteries

www.**kidsatrandomhouse**.co.uk

The Lady Grace Mysteries

FEUD

Grace Cavendish

Patricia Finney is writing as Grace Cavendish

DOUBLEDAY
London • New York • Toronto • Sydney • Auckland

THE LADY GRACE MYSTERIES: FEUD
A DOUBLEDAY BOOK 0 385 60851 9

Published in Great Britain by Doubleday,
an imprint of Random House Children's Books

This edition published 2005

1 3 5 7 9 10 8 6 4 2

Series created by Working Partners Ltd
Copyright © Working Partners Ltd, 2005
Cover illustration by David Wyatt

Papers used by Random House Children's Books are natural, recyclable products
made from wood grown in sustainable forests. The manufacturing processes
conform to the environmental regulations of the country of origin.

Set in Bembo by Palimpsest Book Production Limited, Polmont, Stirlingshire

RANDOM HOUSE CHILDREN'S BOOKS
61–63 Uxbridge Road, London W5 5SA
A division of The Random House Group Ltd

RANDOM HOUSE AUSTRALIA (PTY) LTD
20 Alfred Street, Milsons Point, Sydney,
New South Wales 2061, Australia

RANDOM HOUSE NEW ZEALAND LTD
18 Poland Road, Glenfield, Auckland 10, New Zealand

RANDOM HOUSE (PTY) LTD
Endulini, 5A Jubilee Road, Parktown 2193, South Africa

THE RANDOM HOUSE GROUP Limited Reg. No. 954009
www.**kids**at**randomhouse**.co.uk

A CIP catalogue record for this book
is available from the British Library.

Printed and bound in Great Britain by
Clays Ltd, St Ives plc

To Anita Wilce — a.k.a.
Nanny Nita — with many thanks

Thank you to colours expert
Victoria Finlay for all her advice on
Elizabethan paints and pigments

Most Secrete

The Daybooke of my Lady Grace
Cavendish, Maid of Honour to
Her Gracious Majesty
Queen Elizabeth I

At the Palace of Nonsuch

The First Day of March, in the Year of Our Lord 1570

Near eleven of the clock

A new daybooke! With clean pages and no blots at all! The Queen gave it me this morning and laughed and said I must be the greatest consumer of paper and goose feathers outside the men of the Exchequer and Sir William Cecil himself. She added that I had better leave off my scribbling when I was wed, for what would my husband say when he saw I had scribbled over the accounts?

I curtsied and answered, 'Then I had rather not be wed, so I need not leave the Court and can stay with you, Your Majesty. Especially if I must reckon up accounts as well.' I distinctly saw Lady Jane sniff and toss her head as if she thought I was lying to flatter Her Majesty, because Lady Jane is on fire to marry, I know not why. But the Queen smiled and also gave me a whole bag of goose feathers, already cured and stripped and ready for me to cut into pens, and a new bottle of the best ink from the stationers at St Paul's. That made Mrs Champernowne, Mistress of the Maids, tut and roll her eyes, for fear I would get ink on my kirtle. But then I unwrapped the third part of the present, and found it was a black satin apron backed with canvas so as to be ink-proof, which I knew would please the old Welsh fusspot.

That was early this morning, when we attended Her Majesty after breakfast. Now the sun is high and alas, I am *bored*. Here I am, sitting on a hard cushion in the Presence Chamber, while one of the Scottish Ambassadors proses away at the Queen in that strange language of theirs that almost sounds like proper English but isn't quite. Not even the Queen speaks Scots. The translator is whispering in an undertone, which is very hard to make out, and even with a translation I have no idea what the Scottish Ambassador is going on about, except that it has something to do with the scandalous Queen of Scots.

Mary Shelton is knitting the second of a pair of silk stockings for herself, while Carmina is embroidering beside me. I ought really to be embroidering as well, but instead I am trying to write this with my new book balanced on my knee and the inkpot on the rush matting next to me.

Mrs Champernowne has already given me a nasty scowl, but I have my new black satin apron on and can ignore her, since it will stop any more disasters striking my kirtle. As if it was my fault that Carmina tripped and knocked my ink bottle flying last week. I did ask if I could perhaps have a black kirtle next time to hide the ink, but the Queen frowned and said it is not always suitable for a Maid of Honour to wear black and thus it would be impractical. Alackaday. Still, the apron will do nicely.

I do like being the youngest Maid of Honour at the Queen's Court. I have been with the Queen for as long as I can remember, and she has been so kind to me since my poor mother died two years ago, saving Her Majesty's life.

But I wish I didn't have to wear suitable raiment all the time. Kirtles, farthingales, petticoats and the like are such a nuisance, especially when I want to go climbing trees with my friends Masou the acrobat and Ellie from the laundry. And there are some wonderful climbing trees here at the Palace of Nonsuch, because we are right out in the Surrey countryside and there is a ring of coppices next the orchards, for supplying the Court with firewood.

Oh no! The first blot.

Later, at the painters' and stainers' workroom

I am waiting for Lady Sarah to change her attire, so I will write a little more of the morning's events. Lord! What a to-do there was! I wish there was a better way of writing than pen and ink, for I nearly lost another white damask kirtle despite my new apron.

And that big blot above wasn't my fault, either. Mary Shelton elbowed me as we sat with the Queen. 'Have you drawn out my embroidery pattern yet?' she whispered. 'I have the heavy linen for the sleeves now.'

I sighed, put my newly smudged book down to dry, for I had no wiper or sand to blot it, and then fished about in my workbag. It is in terrible disorder, I fear, what with all the old quills and scraps of paper – and my penner. I keep my embroidery work in another bag inside it to keep it from getting dirty.

Mary's pattern was right at the bottom. 'Here it is,' I said at last, uncrumpling it and showing it to her.

'Oh!' said Mary Shelton, with a big smile across her pleasant, round face. 'Oh, that's lovely!'

I felt myself going pink. I did try hard with the pattern because I like Mary, even though she snores. I had made a simple trellis-work design with curling branches for most of the blackwork, but for the centres of the diamond shapes I drew a little picture of a cat carrying a kitten and peeping out from behind a rose. I did it from memory: a little while ago the

Cook in the Privy Kitchen found a mother cat with kittens in one of the wood boxes by the fire.

'Ahh,' cooed Mary in delight, taking it from me. 'Look here, Carmina, isn't it just like Grimalkin in the Privy Kitchen?'

'Hmm? Eh?' muttered Carmina, who had been dozing where she sat. Small blame to her: that Ambassador's miserable whining voice would put anyone to sleep. It would serve him right if the Queen herself started to snore, not that she would. She always looks sharply at ambassadors and listens to every word. I don't know how she does it.

'I'll draw it again on thicker paper, so you can make pinholes to pounce it for the embroidery and repeat the pattern,' I said. 'Mayhap Mrs Teerlinc will give me some when I go to the painters' workroom this noontide.'

Lady Sarah overheard this. She had been sitting a little further off, pointedly ignoring Lady Jane, who is very full of herself because she has a new admirer, and chatting to Penelope Knollys about a new way of charming spots off your nose. 'Oh no,' she groaned. 'Not again.'

'The Queen said we had to go back again today, did I not tell you?' I said, a little defensively because of course I had forgotten.

'I thought they had finished painting all those tedious great portraits,' moaned Sarah. I cannot understand why she doesn't like going.

'No,' I said. 'There is another batch to be done of the Queen's Majesty, and you must wear a different set of robes for her.'

Lady Sarah sighed dramatically. 'If only I didn't look so like the Queen,' she muttered.

'It can't be as bad as all that,' said Penelope a little enviously. She's a pale slip of a thing, and always takes Lady Sarah's advice on colours to wear. Today she has new beeswax with crushed New World beetles in it on her lips to make them pink. She has some on her front teeth and it looks terrible.

'Huh, you have no idea!' snapped Lady Sarah, with a toss of her red curls. 'It's perfectly awful having to stand stock-still in that horrible smelly workroom. And the Queen's bodices are always too tight for me, so I can hardly breathe and feel near to fainting. And if I so much as move a finger that fat Dutchwoman tells me off for it.' She turned an accusing stare on me. 'And *then* the person who's *supposed* to be reading to me, to keep me from *dying* of boredom, is usually *poking* around talking to that young limner, Nick Hillman—'

'Hilliard,' I told her.

'Whatever, and scribbling and asking questions and doing anything except getting on with reading the story, and—' said Sarah, heaving her bosom magnificently even though there were no young gentlemen to admire it, except Sir William Cecil and the Scottish Ambassadors, who certainly do not count. She broke off because I kicked her. I had seen Her Majesty looking at us – Lady Sarah was whispering too loudly.

'Your sufferings must be dreadful,' sniffed Lady Jane, who hadn't noticed that the Queen was watching.

Carmina's head had been hanging over her embroidery again, and now she gave such an amazing pig's grunt that even the Ambassador hesitated for a second, and the Queen's eyes narrowed in fury. We all started giggling – we couldn't help it – as Carmina gave another very loud snore. It sounded like a mixture of a wood saw and somebody drowning, to be honest.

A slipper whizzed past Carmina's head and Mary Shelton shook her arm.

'Eh?' queried Carmina, waking up with a start.

'Mistress Willoughby, had you rather go to your bed than attend upon us?' rapped out the Queen in a terrible voice.

Poor Carmina stumbled to her feet, bright red with embarrassment, and curtsied. 'I am so sorry, Your Majesty,' she stuttered. 'I don't know what's wrong with me; I cannot seem to keep awake.'

'Are you distempered?' There was a nasty edge to the Queen's voice – she gets very cross if we have too much spiced wine in the evening, making us heavy and stupid and distempered of drink the next day.

'I have a megrim, Your Majesty, but I thought it might go away,' Carmina replied. 'I am sure

I am not distempered, for I only had some small beer yesterday and only ale and a sweet-meat for breakfast.'

The Queen's scowl softened; she is always very kind when one of us is ill.

'Now, I'm sure Mrs Champernowne has told you that if you feel unwell you must stay in bed,' she said, not scolding very much. 'My Lady Horsley, would you do me the favour of helping Carmina to her bed, and save Mrs Champernowne's rheumatism?'

Lady Horsley is a thin, bony lady with a tired face, not long come to Court. She was with the other Ladies-in-Waiting on the other side of the room, and she put down her work at once and stood. 'Of course, Your Majesty,' she said in a soft, gentle voice. 'Come along, Carmina, my dear. I'll make you up a tisane to help your head.'

Carmina smiled gratefully at her and left the room, leaning on her arm.

'No doubt it is the cares of her wonderful new inheritance that are keeping her awake at night,' said Lady Jane spitefully. Luckily for her, the Queen was concentrating on the Scots Ambassador again and did not hear.

Mary Shelton tutted as she cast off her knitting and shook her head. 'What nonsense,' she whispered to me. 'It's only the single manor of Chigley with a few villages . . .'

'And then you put the crushed woodlice on your nose, turn around three times and say . . .' Lady Sarah was muttering to Penelope, who was nodding wisely. They may have little in common, but they do both have spots.

'Can none of you stop jabbering for a second?' snapped the Queen. The Ambassador stopped in mid-moan, the translator stuttered and Sir William smiled that blank, meaningless smile of his. It suddenly occurred to me that the Queen is really just as bored as we are, save she is better at hiding it. We all sat still as stone and stared at the Queen.

'God's blood, I swear you would try the patience of God Almighty Himself!' she shouted, looking for something to throw. 'Whisper, whisper, jabber, jabber, twitter, twitter like a parcel of hens! And Lady Sarah, did I not tell you to go to Mrs Teerlinc in the workroom for another sitting?'

'Well, I . . .' began Sarah, standing and curtsying and going rather red.

'I am so sorry, Your Majesty,' I said, jumping up myself. 'It's my fault. I forgot to tell her— Oh, no! Hell's teeth!'

It was my pot of ink. I had tipped it over. I grabbed it up quickly, but there was a pool of ink soaking into the rush matting, and of course all the girls in their white damask kirtles were squealing and wailing and scrambling out of the way. Then Mrs Champernowne bustled over, despite her rheumatism, tutting and telling me off for swearing, and beckoning one of the gentlemen to fetch a Chamberer with a cloth, and, well . . . You'd think there had been a snake or a scorpion loose in the room, really you would. I stood there, holding the ink bottle, not really knowing what to do. And then I saw the Queen shake her head and grin at me secretly, before becoming all stern again.

'Really!' she said. 'If you cannot even sit like sensible ladies, then all of you may leave. Go on, off with you! Lady Grace, will you please put the stopper in your ink bottle? Else we shall have yet another disaster, and I shall repent me of ever giving it to you or having you taught to write. You may accompany Lady Sarah to the workroom to read to her and the rest of you – shoo!' So we lined up to curtsy, and she shouted at us as we left, 'And stay clear of the damned players too!'

We all trooped out to the antechamber, where the gentlemen were playing dice. Lady Jane was tutting at me and Penelope was too, and Sarah rolled her eyes until Mary Shelton said sensibly, 'Well, I think the Queen was just looking for an excuse to get rid of us. And I think Lady Grace has saved us all, because that Scot looked like he was settling in for another two hours at least!'

'Poor Queen,' said I. 'She has to sit there and listen. But what did she mean about the players?'

Everybody looked at everybody else. 'Perchance the Master of the Revels has asked a band of players for to entertain the Scots Ambassador?' suggested Penelope.

When Lady Jane was quite certain she had no specks on her kirtle, she went off with Penelope to investigate the matter of the players. Meanwhile, Mary Shelton went to visit Carmina, and I went with Lady Sarah – who was still complaining about the Queen's bodices being too tight – and Mrs Champernowne, who was rubbing her back where it ached with the change in the weather.

We had to go to the Outer Courtyard to get to the limners and stainers' workroom. (Lady Jane told me that in France it would be called an 'atelier', but the Queen will have no truck with such Frenchified stuff and nor will I.) We had to climb a great many stairs, for it is on the very top floor, one side overlooking the court, the other overlooking the orchard at the rear of Nonsuch, planted by the Queen's father, King Henry.

And so that's where I am now. There is a workroom at Whitehall as well, but this is newly set up so that Mistress Teerlinc can properly supervise the Queen's portraits while we are in Surrey. We arrived and curtsied to Mrs Teerlinc, who is a kind, plump lady with a Netherlander accent. It is amazing how much she laughs and shakes her shoulders – she has been a gentle-woman at Court since Her Majesty was a princess, and so must be terribly old. She is wearing the most beautiful, spring-green silk gown, with not the smallest speck of paint on it anywhere. I wonder how on earth she does it!

There is a great deal of puffing going on behind the screen, where Mrs Champernowne is helping Sarah to dress. It's true that the Queen's bodices are much narrower than Sarah's and it seems to be taking a tremendous amount of heaving by Mrs Champernowne – and sucking in and holding her breath by Sarah – to get the stay laces fastened.

The workroom is a high-ceilinged room, all whitewashed, with large windows fitted with glass to let in more light, though that means the room is always very cold. The floorboards are bare, not covered with rushes or mats, so that the easels can stand steady holding the stretched canvases upon frames – and wooden panels too for the better quality paintings. There are five easels set up – as many as can fit round the dais – all with part-begun paintings of the Queen in her robes. It would be terribly foolish to paint only one at a time as there is such a demand for them. Every town hall in England wants one. And ever since the Queen saw a portrait of herself which, as she put it, made her look 'like a half-witted strumpet from the South Bank', she has insisted that all must come from the palace and be approved by her. So there is a never-ending stream of portraits being painted, and mayors are always trying to bribe their way up the waiting list.

There are sinks and counters on both sides of the room, where the apprentices and journeymen grind and mix the paints. Further back, there are wooden arches being painted for a masque, and designs for another bodice for the Queen, and some first outlinings for tapestries. The workroom does smell very strange – of turpentine and oils and the things they use for colours – but it is a fascinating place to be. Unfortunately, Lady Sarah is not much interested, except in the designs for kirtles and gowns, which is a shame as she must stand in for the Queen so often. She has just come out from behind the screen, fully arrayed in the Queen's gown – which I must admit looks well on her, even if it is too tight. And now I must start reading to her so she will stay still.

Early afternoon, in our chamber

I think that was a wonderful morning, no matter what Lady Sarah might say. Mrs Champernowne left as soon as Sarah was ready in the Queen's robes, which are most magnificent in black and white velvet and brocade, and heavy with pearls and jewels of all kinds.

The five painter-stainers were preparing their palettes with odd-smelling pigments. They all wore smudged brown smocks to protect their clothes. Three were quite old – at least forty! Another was very old and grey. The last was Nick Hilliard, who is tall and slim but has the remains of a black eye.

I happen to know he got it in a tavern brawl ten days ago because Ellie told me all about it. She heard of it from one of the other laundry-maids who knows a lad who works in the stable, who has a friend in the smithy whose brother was in the tavern when Nick got the black eye. She said that Nick was playing cards and boast-ing of all the money he would make – because he has next to none at present – when he got himself a patron with his latest great classical painting. One of the other card players said he couldn't wait that long for his money, and Nick said he didn't pay cheats! So the other man hit him and there was a big brawl, which broke up the game. And that was just as well, Ellie said, because the cards were marked and Nick was too drunk to know it. 'An' it served him right to get his eye blacked,' she added darkly, 'for not knowing what a terrible cony-catcher that man is and 'ow you shouldn't play him at anything – 'specially not cards and dice.'

I looked cautiously at Nick, who had looked well enough for a drinking man.

He caught me looking at him and smiled ruefully, touching his cheekbone. 'Do you like my battle scar, my lady?' he asked.

'I heard you got it in a fight over a card game,' I said. 'Is that true?'

'In a way,' he admitted. 'Lord knows, some men get very impatient for their money. Do you like to play?'

'I play a little Primero with the Queen sometimes,' I told him. 'But she generally gives me the money to play in the first place.'

He smiled again, and shook his head. 'But where's the excitement in that,' he asked, 'if you can afford to lose?'

I didn't know what to say to that.

Lady Sarah, who was perched on a stool on the little dais, sighed, and I remembered I was supposed to be reading to her. I had a new book about brave warriors and magical lands and a quest for a magic sword.

Mrs Teerlinc went to her desk in the corner and began to cast up her accounts with an abacus and a long list of bills. I tried to watch her, as I read aloud, to discover how she could write accounts with pen and ink and still not get ink on her at all.

Mrs Teerlinc is the Head Limner at Court and has a pension from the Queen, so all the other limners are very jealous of her, especially as she is a woman. Because of her position she has very little time for painting, so she mainly does beautiful, tiny portraits and pictures on vellum stuck to playing cards.

It's the very latest thing to have a little miniature portrait of your love to carry with you. Daft gentlemen are always saying they want to carry Lady Sarah's beauteous visage next their devoted hearts. Ha!

I tried to concentrate on reading. The book is translated from the French and has some very long words in it. I quite like romances, if only they could get to the fighting sooner and leave out some of the description of the beauteous lady's golden locks, wondrous samite gowns and tiny feet clad in Cordova leather and so on. Of course, Lady Sarah loves those parts.

I read and read, but I also kept looking up to see Nick Hilliard painting. It is very interesting, for his face is intent, like a cat watching a bird before pouncing, and his hand moves so fast with the brush. It is as if he can't paint fast enough to catch the colours in front of him.

Lady Sarah was scowling at me, her cheeks pink from wearing the Queen's heavy robes, and I realized that watching Nick Hilliard had stopped me from reading. So I started again hastily.

'You've read that bit,' she snapped crossly. 'Twice!'

I coughed, skipped a paragraph and read on. One of the stainers tutted because Sarah started fanning herself with the Queen's ostrich feather fan instead of staying still.

Mrs Teerlinc had finished her accounts and now had her hand on the shoulder of the stainer, who was painting nearest to me. He was an old man with a tangled grey beard and eyebrows like birds' nests. He squinted at Sarah, and then screwed his eyes up close to the panel he was painting, as if he could hardly see what he was doing. I thought the pupils of his eyes looked odd, as if there was milk in them.

'I think you should rest your eyes now, Ned,' said Mrs Teerlinc. 'You go for your pipe and a bit to eat.'

'Ay, well,' he said. 'My eyes are tired. Maybe the morning mist will have cleared when I come back.' He cleaned his fingers on a rag, tucked the brushes into the easel so they wouldn't touch anything else and went out of the workroom.

Mrs Teerlinc looked at his painting and sighed. 'Nick, my dear,' she said sadly, looking at some mistakes in Ned's painting, 'would you mind?'

Nick came over from his own easel, bringing his palette and brushes. He scowled at Ned's painting. Then he grabbed a brush and worked like lightning, painting right over Ned's mistakes – which you can do with paints that are mixed with oil, for they don't run at all.

The result was so much better. As Nick used his colours, and lit the shine of the pearls with silver in resin, the jewels seemed to grow there on the panel, hanging on the bodice like the real jewels! I thought they almost glinted as Her Majesty breathed.

'Oh, really, Grace!' snapped Sarah. 'Please will you stop *stopping*?'

Guiltily, I returned to reading some very elaborate speeches about lady-loves while occasionally sneaking glances at Nick Hilliard's work. I read about the terrible dragon and the beauteous lady in its clutches, and I tried to concentrate, but every so often I'd forget to read as I watched jewels and pearls and brocade spring up from Nick's brushes as if burning through the wood panel.

By the time Ned came back, smelling of that horrible henbane of Peru that some people smoke to cure their phlegm, Nick had finished reworking all the painting the old man had done that morning and was back at his own easel, looking as if butter wouldn't melt in his mouth.

I remembered Mary Shelton's embroidery pattern and forgot all about reading again. 'May I have some heavy paper for pouncing?' I asked.

'Of course,' said Mrs Teerlinc, and she beckoned one of the two apprentices to bring some scrap paper to me. 'You Maids certainly do a great deal of embroidery work,' she added.

'Well, it is the only way we can make pictures with colours,' I explained, a little sadly for I would love to do some painting myself. 'I wish I could learn to paint with the beautiful, bright colours you use.'

Mrs Teerlinc smiled and shook her head. 'Ah, no,' she said. 'I'm afraid they are too valuable. The blue for the sky is made of ground lapis lazuli. Besides, it takes years to learn how to use all the colours. And at least embroidery silks will not stain your kirtle.'

'No, thank the Lord, or I would never have a clean one!' I declared ruefully. 'I have trouble enough with pen and ink.'

'Grace,' moaned Sarah. 'What happens next? Stop chatting about drawing and painting and read to me.'

But Mrs Teerlinc was patting my arm, 'Perhaps I can help,' she said. 'Here is a graphite pen – see, it makes only a grey dust if you brush it. You can write with it and never need to dip your pen in an ink bottle.'

'How wonderful!' I exclaimed. 'It would be marvellous not having to use ink.' Of course

I tried it – and that is what I am writing with now! No ink at all!

'You can draw with it too,' Mrs Teerlinc added with a smile, and gave me two more graphite pens from her little table which I put straight in my penner. 'Now be careful with them, for they are quite easy to break and *very* expensive, so I will not be able to give you more.'

'*Gra-a-ace!*' moaned Sarah. 'What happens with the dragon?'

So I sat there for another hour, reading out long speeches from the beauteous damsel, and even longer speeches from the brave knight who rescued her.

At last the Queen's kirtle was done and we could leave. I helped Sarah change her clothes again – it's lucky she doesn't mind doing that, at least. It is terribly fiddly: lifting off the heavy gown and putting it on its stand, unlacing the sleeves and drawing them off, unhooking the bodice down the side, and then unhooking the back of the kirtle and taking that off. Finally, I untied the Queen's stay laces so that

Sarah could stand in her shift and bumroll and farthingale and sigh and breathe again. And then, of course, I had to do her up again in her own stays and bodice and kirtle. It's agonizingly boring, wearing fine clothes, really it is. I wish I were like Ellie and could put one thing on in the morning and then wear it all day. In fact, I don't think she even puts it on in the morning. I think she just wears it day and night until it falls apart or she grows out of it and has to find a new kirtle.

I went back to the parlour for a bite of dinner with Lady Sarah. Olwen was waiting for us, and Sarah decided I hadn't been very good as a tiring woman, so after we ate, she had Olwen dress her all over again. But the good thing was that I managed to sneak a little time in my chamber to try out my new graphite pen. And so here I am, and this pen is a wonder of the world, for it never blots or runs at all!

Mary Shelton has just come in from visiting Carmina, who has a terrible megrim, poor soul, and was not with us for dinner. 'Penelope says there is to be a play tonight in honour of the Scottish Ambassadors!' Mary has just said excitedly. 'And Her Majesty desires you to walk the dogs, Lady Grace.'

So, off I go.

In the evening after supper, in my chamber

Lady Sarah and Mary Shelton are painting their faces and readying themselves to see the play. I am ready now, so I have time to write in my daybooke.

I changed into my old hunting kirtle, put my graphite pens into the petticoat pocket, with my daybooke and some sugared almonds for Ellie, and then ran on tiptoe downstairs and along the Painted Passage to the door to the Privy Garden, where a Chamberer was waiting with the dogs.

There were a couple of carts just coming into the Outer Courtyard. People were rushing about and the Master of the Revels arrived, looking very pompous in his velvet gown with his white wand of office, to talk to the handsome middle-aged man sitting on the lead cart. Both carts seemed to be full of brightly coloured cloth and I wondered what on earth they were come for, but then I remembered the play. I would have stayed to watch the players prepare but I had promised Masou I would see him as soon as I could and walking the dogs gave me the perfect opportunity to meet him and Ellie.

I went through the orchard, towards the new buildings. Because the village of Epsom is too small to take everyone connected with the Court, extra housing has been built. There are still not enough chambers for everyone: some people have to take haylofts and attics in the village, others just camp wherever they can. The richest lords have chambers near the Queen or stay at houses they have built nearby. It's always a problem finding lodging space for everybody who wants to come to Court and make their fortune by catching the Queen's eye. All the young men complain about how expensive it is, and how they have to share rooms and servants, but still they come.

At the farthest end of the orchard the wall has tumbled down and it is easy to climb over. I did so, with the dogs yapping excitedly and lifting their legs against the stones, and jumped down into the nearest coppice. The wood will not be cut for another year or two, so it is nice and thick with trees.

Masou was waiting for me in the den he and Ellie have made by curving the withies over and tying them at the top, and then covering them with dry branches. It is quite hard to see in from the outside, except that Masou's suit of coloured patches shows a little through the branches.

'Ellie will be along in a moment, only Her Majesty's silk woman asked her to help with some partlets and a veil,' said Masou. 'And I, who am merely the best tumbler in Mr Somers's troupe, am not at all important and may be kept waiting by players and their stupid carts!'

He usually has a smile on his face when he

says something like that, so I was surprised to see he was really quite cross.

'Lord, Masou, what's to do?' I asked.

'Hmph!' said he. 'Players, players, nought but players. They have been here in the village two days awaiting their scenery, for they said they cannot play without it — as if we had none!'

Aha, I thought, that is why we did not know of them before — they were not yet properly come to Court.

Masou was still grumbling. 'They lost two axles in a pothole on the road from London, and had to have them mended, but they finally came today, alas. And the way they strut about as if they were pashas . . . Ptah!' And he spat on the ground in disgust.

I wanted to experiment some more with my lovely graphite pens, so I settled down with my daybooke on my knees and started to draw Masou. It was very difficult to limn him, especially as he would not stay still. He was tossing red and green leather balls up and about his head, and I drew them too, like a halo for an old saint in a church window. It was hard to get the shine on his cheek, but one of the good things about graphite is that you can smudge it with your finger, so at last I had something I thought was nearly good.

Masou looked at my drawing. He said something in his own language and grinned. 'Wonderful,' he translated for me. 'Though my father told me that a true Mussulman never makes pictures of living things, for that is God's privilege.'

'What do the kings decorate their palaces with then?' I asked curiously.

'Our writing – which is very graceful and beautiful, like the wind patterns in the sand. I have seen whole walls covered in it.'

He took one of the graphite sticks and carefully drew a sort of curly shape on the paper. You could tell it was writing, even if there was no way of making sense of it. He told me it was his name – and then he rubbed it out with his finger and some spit, so no one could make a charm out of it and enchant him.

We heard singing coming through the thick bushes, and suddenly Ellie pushed her way into the bower, bright-eyed and happy. 'Now then, Masou,' she said, 'are you still as snippy as you was this morning at the buttery?'

Masou scowled and sniffed loudly.

'Oops, I shouldn't 'ave reminded him,' grinned Ellie, elbowing me painfully. 'He's jealous.'

I sighed because Masou was now looking as sour as before I did his picture.

'I see no good reason why a performance we have been practising for two weeks should be cancelled just because some starveling, pig-eating mummers catch the eye of the Master of the Revels and so are hired to make exhibition of their stupidity!' Masou declared, very haughty.

'That's a good likeness of 'im,' interrupted Ellie, catching sight of my limning. ''Cept for the nose, o' course.'

Masou suddenly stopped talking about the terrible players; he looked confused and rubbed his nose. 'Why? What's wrong with it?' he demanded.

Ellie munched the sugared almonds I'd brought her and dug me in the ribs again with her very sharp elbow. 'It is a pity about 'is nose, ain't it?' she said to me, winking.

'Yes, it is,' I agreed, looking as serious as I could. 'It's terrible.'

'Dunno what could of 'appened to do that to it,' Ellie went on, shaking her head. 'Must be them players . . .'

'What?' demanded Masou, crossing his eyes in an effort to look at his nose.

'Yes,' I sighed, sucking the last sugared almond. 'I think the players did the damage.'

'*What damage?*' hissed Masou, looking annoyed and worried at the same time. 'Is there a pimple? What have they done?'

'Put your nose out of joint, o' course, you great ninny!' Ellie shrieked, and started laughing. And so did I, I'm afraid, because Masou looked so cross. 'Your nose is so out of joint it's round the other side of your head!'

'Honestly,' I said, as Masou started throwing leaves and bits of earth at us. 'Aren't you pleased to get a night off and the chance to watch a new play?'

'I heard it's very good,' said Ellie. 'Susannah

at the laundry said she saw it at the Bel Savage Inn, Ludgate, last week and it's wonderful. And as for that Richard Fitzgrey—'

'Who?' asked Masou and I together.

Ellie leaned closer, grinning with mischief. 'Oh, he'll put all your delicate Maids of Honour in a fluster all right. Course, he's really called Dickon Greyson, but 'e likes to fancy 'e's secretly a lord's son' – she winked – 'so 'e calls 'isself Richard Fitzgrey.'

Masou and I looked at each other. I shook my head. 'I don't think a poor travelling player will make much progress with Lady Sarah or Lady Jane,' I said. 'They know they've got to marry rich nobles . . .'

Ellie wagged a finger at me. 'You wait,' she said. 'You'll see.' And with that, she jumped up. 'Come on, I'll show you. They're setting up in the Great Hall right now.'

Masou sniffed. 'I've seen all I need to,' he snapped. 'We shall soon see how they compare with skilled acrobats.'

So Ellie and I left him there and climbed back over the wall. It took a while to round up the dogs, who had been trying to catch rabbits and were all covered with mud, but at last we had them leashed. I gave Ellie the leashes, so that I could say we were taking the dogs to the laundry courtyard to wash them down, and give her a good reason to be with me.

We passed by the back steps to the Great Hall and there were the players unloading one of the carts, carrying poles and bundles of coloured cloth in across the Outer Courtyard. One of them was standing on the cart in his shirtsleeves and waistcoat, shouting orders at two boys who were struggling with a huge bundle.

Ellie nodded. 'There 'e is,' she whispered. 'Richard Fitzgrey hisself.'

I looked at him. Well, he is tall and has that sort of triangular shape all the gentlemen at Court either have, or try to fake by having the shoulders of their doublets padded. He has a long jaw, bright blue eyes and black hair worn long about his ears.

Then I noticed something soppy about Ellie's expression. 'Isn't he gorgeous?' she said.

'Well, I suppose he's all right,' I admitted reluctantly. His flashing blue eyes are certainly attractive. But he did look rather big-headed.

Ellie elbowed me again. 'Oh, you!' she giggled. 'Don't 'e tickle your fancy even a little?'

And then I saw a very funny thing. Lady Sarah and Penelope were crossing the court-yard together, arm in arm. I could tell that Sarah had pulled her stomacher down as far as she could, and her hair was doing that thing where it's pinned up perfectly under her little green hat, but a few red ringlets seem to be falling down. It takes her ages and ages in front of the mirror to make her hair do that and somehow it makes young gentlemen's brains go soggy – at least, it seems to when Lady Sarah does it. She was smiling and laughing at something Penelope was saying.

The unloading stopped. The two boys stood staring with the enormous bundle of cloth in their arms, and Richard Fitzgrey vaulted straight down from the cart and swept off his hat to the ladies, in the most elegant, courtly bow you can imagine.

Both Sarah and Penelope seemed to think this was terribly witty and giggled as they walked past.

Then all of a sudden Lady Jane appeared holding a posy of crocuses and swaying elegantly as she walked in the opposite direction. She was wearing her most fashionable Parisian gown, and pretending to ignore Richard completely – though I saw her watching him out of the corner of her eye. And then, good heavens, there was Lettice Knollys, Penelope's pretty aunt, casually strolling along, followed by two of Her Majesty's Lady Chamberers!

From being empty, the courtyard was suddenly full of women – which was quite a coincidence, because there weren't that many women at Nonsuch. Most of the people at Court are men – and I noticed that none of *them* seemed to find the unloading of the players' scenery anything like as fascinating as the ladies did.

Ellie was very proper now, standing behind me and stopping the muddy dogs from going over and lifting their legs on the cartwheels. But she did look up at one of the upper windows.

I followed the line of her gaze, and there was Mrs Champernowne, shaking out a napkin from an upstairs window. What could she be doing there? Was she . . . ? Could she be . . . ? Surely she was too old!

Richard Fitzgrey spotted her and waved cheekily and I swear she went bright red as she accidentally dropped the napkin. I nearly exploded with laughter.

Richard jumped back onto the cart and started directing the others again – though I must say, if he was so strong and clever, why wasn't he carrying some of the heavy things himself?

I led on, with Ellie sneaking quick glances at Richard over her shoulder as we went. We took the dogs round the back to the laundry courtyard, where there's a pump, and managed to get them washed down a bit. Then I went inside and gave them to the Chamberer who usually feeds them.

I was just hurrying back to my chamber when Mrs Champernowne caught me.

'Goodness gracious! What have you been up to, Lady Grace?' she spluttered. 'Your kirtle is soaked through, look you.'

'I got splashed a little while we were cleaning the dogs after their walk,' I said very demurely. 'Didn't you see how muddy they were when you were shaking your napkin out of the window?'

Mrs Champernowne looked flustered. 'Well, get on with you and change,' she said. 'What are you doing dripping and drizzling all over the tiles?'

I'm sure I can't see what all the fuss is over Richard Fitzgrey. And now Mary Shelton wants to know why I'm scribbling again instead of changing into my best gown. She says even Carmina is getting up to see the play, because she heard from Penelope how well-looking that player is. *Honestly!*

And now Fran is chivvying me too, and saying I have not brushed my hair, when I did it just this morning!

Later, in my bed

When I went down with the other Maids for the play, I saw that all the long tables had been cleared from the Great Hall, and the benches set in rows so we could sit and watch the players on the stage they had built. Mary Shelton came down with Carmina leaning on her arm. She was looking very concerned, because Carmina was as white as a sheet and very tired.

Then Lady Jane and Lady Sarah appeared, ignoring each other haughtily. Jane was in her finest French-style kirtle, a very pale kind of blue satin damask, and Sarah in a wonderful new gown of forest-green velvet, trimmed with gold braid, her hair tumbling down around her ears. I don't know why she complains so much about the Queen's stays being tight, for she has her own so tight it is a wonder she does not pop out the top. The two of them sat down, with Penelope between them. She looked like a little brown mouse in her tawny velvet.

Lady Jane rolled her eyes at me and smiled in that annoyingly superior way she has. 'Did you know that with you in your rose velvet and Carmina in crimson, your gowns are clashing terribly?' she said to me. 'Why not have Lady Sarah sit beside you so her hair can join the fun?'

Lady Sarah tossed her hair so the ringlets bounced. 'At least mine is the same colour as the Queen's,' she sniffed, and Lady Jane looked daggers at her.

Meanwhile the Scottish Ambassadors arrived and sat in a row, looking like pints of vinegar, they were so sour with disapproval at the heathen mumming, which is what they call playing.

The Queen arrived last of all and sat on her throne, which had been turned about so that she could see the dais. Everybody knelt until she waved at us to sit down. Then the trumpets sounded and the players bounded onto the stage to bow and then launch into the prologue. You might have thought there were a lot of them, but in fact all the parts were played by just two middle-aged men, Richard Fitzgrey, three younger men and three boys.

The play was long and very complicated, all about two families who hate each other. There's a huge massacre of one family by the other. Only one young man is left – wounded but alive. The princess of the enemy family finds him, takes him in and nurses him without knowing who he is. Of course she falls in love with him, but then he realizes that he's in the heart of his enemy's castle. So he disguises himself as a servant and puts poison in the wine. Only by now he's in love with the beauteous princess, and she's the one who goes to drink the poisoned wine! So the young man drinks it himself too, and then declares his love in a very, very long speech, before dying tragically.

I don't think somebody dying would be able to go on about his love for *quite* so long, but Richard did it very well – you could hear every word and all the Maids were sniffling, even Lady Jane.

Oh – except for Carmina, who was sitting next to me. She fell asleep with her head on my shoulder about three-quarters of the way through, when it was just getting really exciting. She wouldn't wake up even though I pinched her. I was scared she'd snore again and get us all sent out.

The Queen didn't cry at the end, of course, but she did clap a lot. The players danced a Bergomask afterwards, which turned into a kind of riot because of the antics of one of the men as a clown. That made us all laugh again. The Master of the Revels then brought the chief of the company, the good-looking middle-aged man I had seen earlier, and Richard Fitzgrey, to be presented to Her Majesty. I distinctly heard four sighs from Mary, Sarah, Jane and Penelope as Richard knelt before Her Majesty, looking much more noble and heroic in his velvet doublet than most of the Court gentlemen.

'Your Majesty, may I present Mr Tom Alleyn and Richard Fitzgrey,' intoned the Master of the Revels.

'Well done indeed,' said the Queen. 'We are well pleased with your playing.' She nodded to the Master of the Revels, who gave Alleyn a leather purse that chinked. Immediately, all the players' expressions went from worried to happy. Then she looked quizzically at Richard Fitzgrey.

'I think all the gentlemen of my Court are jealous of you, Mr Fitzgrey, since you seem to have charmed every single one of my women,' she remarked.

Richard smiled up at her and said, 'Your Gracious Majesty is pleased to praise me, but I rather think that the gentlemen of your Court are jealous because you yourself have deigned to smile on me.'

He couldn't have said a more perfect thing, as the Queen has a great weakness for flattery. All the gentlemen scowled, while even some of the grown-up and married Ladies-in-Waiting sighed this time. Then Richard winked cheekily and the Queen laughed and wagged her finger at him.

'Go to!' she scolded. 'You are very forward!'

'But it suits my purpose,' he said frankly, 'for it brings me nearer to Your Majesty.'

She shook her head. 'And I am proof against your charms, Mr Fitzgrey, though I would delight in seeing you play again. Perhaps something less tragical this time. Have you a comedy to show us?'

Richard and Tom Alleyn looked at each other.

'We could play Your Majesty a comedy of Terence, translated by a Cambridge man,' said Alleyn. 'But it is not yet worthy of showing—'

'Then you may have board and bed at Court until it is,' said the Queen decisively. 'Show it to us in a few days' time. We shall look forward to it.' She held out her hand for them to kiss her ring and they backed away, with Tom Alleyn quietly hefting the pouch he held.

All the Maids were very excited at the prospect of another play, but they were being as quiet as they could, in case the Queen noticed and changed her mind.

Meanwhile, I was shaking Carmina awake, so she could be ready to follow the Queen out. She was so sleepy I wondered if she had been secretly drinking aqua vitae, like my Uncle Cavendish does. She leaned heavily on my arm as we walked from the hall, and as soon as we were out in the Inner Courtyard, I waved at Mary to help me get her upstairs to her chamber.

We brought her to the bedchamber she shares with Lady Jane and Penelope, which was tidy since it didn't have Lady Sarah living in it and scattering clothes everywhere. On the table by the bed was a small box of dates stuffed with marchpane, and a bowl of sugared apricots and another of sugar ribbons. Mary and I didn't wait for the tiring woman, but helped Carmina out of her raiment quickly and got her straight into bed without even changing her smock, since she was so tired. Mrs Champernowne arrived just as Mary was tucking Carmina up and I was putting more wood on the fire.

'Dear me,' she said, frowning anxiously as she felt Carmina's forehead. 'Carmina, my dear, I have brought you a little bowl of bread and milk with sugar and nutmeg. Could you eat some perhaps?'

Carmina sat up against the pillow and took the spoon, but only ate a tiny bit before she put it down again. 'I'm sorry,' she said. 'I just can't. My stomach feels odd. Mayhap Grace could pass me one of the sugared apricots . . .'

Mrs Champernowne held the bowl for her and she took one, nibbled it and then lay down again.

'Hm,' said Mrs Champernowne, feeling Carmina's forehead again as if she didn't really believe what she felt.

'There's no fever,' said Mary Shelton quietly, 'or I would have sent for the doctor myself.'

'Yes, indeed,' said Mrs Champernowne. 'But we shall call him anyway if she is no better in the morning, look you.'

When we got back to our own chamber, we found Penelope, Lady Jane and Lady Sarah all twittering over the play. Soon Penelope and Sarah were discussing how desperately dashing and tragical Richard Fitzgrey was in the death scene.

'Such a pity he isn't really a lord,' sighed Lady Sarah. 'He looks wonderful. I wonder how well he can ride.'

'I liked him when he was all wounded and pale and the princess was nursing him without knowing who he really was,' sighed Penelope.

I think they are all Bedlam mad over the player.

'Such a pity — as a player he will never be rich,' continued Lady Sarah. 'If he was a soldier or a sailor, he could sack a city, make his fortune, and then the Queen could make him a lord.'

'Rich?' sniffed Lady Jane. 'He'll be lucky if he never gets put in gaol or whipped for vagrancy.'

The churchmen say that players are only one step removed from beggars, but they don't *look* like vagrants.

'Did you know he can read and write?' said Mary. 'I suppose he has to, so he can learn all the long parts. Perchance he could be a poet.'

'That won't make him rich either,' sniffed Sarah sadly.

I am going to go to sleep as soon as I have finished writing, so I don't have to hear any more wittering about Richard Fitzgrey. I am far more interested in Carmina's sickness. Poor Carmina, I wonder what can be wrong with her. It is such a puzzle for she has no fever at all. I asked Mary Shelton what she thought it could be and she became serious at once.

'I was worried it might be a gaol fever,' Mary said with a sigh. 'Except she hasn't got any fever, so it can't be.'

'Gaol fever!' squeaked Lady Sarah in horror.

'I am sure it is not,' said Mary quickly. 'Though I don't know what else it could be.'

Gaol fever isn't as bad as plague or smallpox but it can easily be deadly – though I don't know how Carmina would have caught it, because she hasn't been near a gaol.

So it *isn't* gaol fever that is making Carmina ill, but nobody seems to know what it *is*. I have no mystery to solve for Her Majesty at present. Perhaps I should investigate whatever is ailing Carmina, since that is become such a puzzle.

But now I'm sleepy and have ink all over my fingers. I did not want to waste my graphite pens when I wasn't wearing my white damask, so there's ink on the sheets too. Hell's teeth! Now Ellie will be cross with me; she hates scrubbing ink stains.

This graphite pen is wonderful, for it never blots at all. I am writing in my daybooke at the workroom while I wait for Mrs Champernowne to help Lady Sarah with the Queen's robes – they have to be arranged perfectly for the portraits.

The Queen is busy with the Scottish Ambassadors again, and thankfully we have all been given this morning free. Mary Shelton said she was going to fetch some comfits for poor Carmina, who is still unwell. She has been ordered by the Queen to stay in bed, though there is still no fever. I was going to go with Mary and see if I could collect any sweetmeats for Ellie and Masou (and myself) when Sarah stopped me in the passage and told me very grumpily that she had to go to the workroom and stand for the Queen's portrait again, and I must go and read to her. So here I am.

Oh, Sarah is ready now so I must stop writing and read. I hope we have more fighting and less speechifying, clothes and lovesickness in the next chapters. I hate it when everyone is so noble and good in a story that you can't imagine it being true at all.

Later, also at the workroom

I have taken the chance to write in my daybooke while all is quiet. Lady Sarah has gone off with Olwen to change and Mrs Teerlinc is casting up her accounts again. If I sit quietly on the window seat and write, they might not notice me. I am using graphite so as not to get any ink on my fingers. The only trouble is that it smudges easily, and I notice that my shift cuffs are going quite grey with it. Never mind, it is still better than ink.

I read to Sarah for ages and received no thanks at all. She was looking out of the big windows a lot and sighing and constantly nibbling at some sugar ribbons she had brought with her. The only time she actually stood still was when the players came out into the courtyard and started practising a swordfight.

I was distracted too, because it was fun to watch them practise a veney with staves instead of swords. Then they changed to blunted blades and did the exact same moves over and over again, speeding up each time.

Meanwhile, old Ned was painting very slowly and squinting hard. Nick Hilliard was doing his own painting at his usual impatient speed, while the other limners discussed cockfighting and painted away carefully.

Then Lady Horsley arrived. She greeted Mrs Teerlinc as an old friend and stood to watch the work. Lady Sarah was fanning herself and scowling again now that Richard Fitzgrey had gone indoors.

Ned left off painting and rubbed his eyes, then squinted at Lady Horsley and looked worried. 'My word,' he said. 'I never saw it was you, my lady.' And he bowed to her.

Lady Horsley nodded kindly at him. 'No

matter, Ned. It is you I came to see, really. How is the henbane of Peru answering to reduce your phlegm?'

'The tabaca? I must say, now I've got used to drinking smoke, I quite like it. And when I think what my old dad paid to put a chimney in the house!' Ned shook his head and chuckled.

'It was recommended me by Dr Nunez, who is a very learned physician,' said Lady Horsley. 'I'm sure it will help.'

'Why don't you go and take a pipe now, Ned?' said Mrs Teerlinc.

'I think I will, thank'ee, ma'am,' he replied, wiping his fingers very carefully before he left.

Mrs Teerlinc waited patiently until we could no longer hear his footsteps and then she nodded at Nick, who shook his head good-humouredly and came over. He shook his head again when he saw old Ned's canvas and then took a small bendy knife and started scraping off nearly everything Ned had done.

'His eyes are no better, you know,' said Mrs Teerlinc to Lady Horsley.

'The smoke-drinking may help if it truly is a problem with his phlegmatic humour, as Dr Cavendish says, but I suspect not . . .' Lady Horsley replied sadly.

'No?'

'I've seen the trouble before,' she continued, sighing. 'The milkiness is in the eye itself, and in the end he will go blind.'

'He nearly is already, my lady,' said Nick sadly. 'Look at this mess.'

Where he was working, the painting was all blurred and smudged as if seen through a dirty glass window.

'I expect that is what he sees,' said Mrs Teerlinc. 'It's a pity he will not retire. The Queen would pay him a good pension, of course, but he says he would have nowhere else to go and nothing to do with himself all day without painting. But this cannot go on. I must think of something we can do for him.'

Sarah sighed again and shifted.

'My lady,' said one of the limners, 'please will you stay still?'

I hastily started reading again – I'm not sure

when I stopped, perhaps when they were talking about henbane of Peru, which is supposed to be a very powerful medicine. I wonder if it would help Carmina. I read right up to the end of the chapter until my throat was quite sore with it. Then Mrs Teerlinc told Sarah she might go and change since all the colours used so far needed to harden.

'Why?' I asked.

'It is a mystery of the trade,' she said, and then smiled when I looked disappointed. 'You see, some colours fight with others and blacken in a year or two. So if one must be laid next to another, the first must harden and be varnished over a little, to protect it from the other.'

I tried to imagine colours fighting each other on a canvas with little swords and spears, which was a very odd thought. I looked at the beautiful yellow colour that Nick was putting down on Ned's picture – the lining of the Queen's Robe of State – and sighed. Then I saw Mrs Teerlinc and Nick exchange a knowing look.

Nick smiled at me. 'Come and try your hand at this, Lady Grace,' he said.

'What?' I gasped. '*Painting?*'

'Of course painting,' he laughed. 'I would need *you* to instruct *me* in embroidery. Come and try it.'

I rushed over as quickly as I could in case he changed his mind. I carefully took his brush, all laden with that wonderful bright yellow paint. Mrs Teerlinc tutted, swept across the room, took the brush out of my hand and put a big canvas apron over me. Then she smiled and gave me the brush back.

'Now,' said Nick, 'see how you get on with the yellow ground here. Just lay it on in the shape I have done in charcoal. Have no fear if you make a mistake, for I can take it off again with my palette knife.'

I squinted my eyes a little and started dabbing carefully. Sarah came back, having changed into her own clothes, and I never even noticed. I barely saw her leave, but I heard her saying something about needing to take the air in the courtyard where the players are at practise again, and Olwen replied, 'Yes, my lady,' very cynically. Lady Horsley went with them,

I think, but she moves very quietly so sometimes you don't realize she's there at all.

After a short time I thought I had finished. Nick looked at what I had done and announced that it was 'Passing excellent for a novice!' I was very pleased.

I noticed Sarah had left a little pile of broken sugar ribbons by the high stool she had been using. All the concentrating had made me very hungry, so I wandered over to the pile of sugar ribbons and picked one up to nibble on it—

Suddenly someone swooped up behind me and knocked it out of my hand. I swung round to see who it was and found it was Mrs Teerlinc. I was so surprised I just stared.

'Really, Lady Grace, do you not like your life?' she asked, and she was almost shouting, which is most unlike her – she is usually so friendly and kind. So I stood there, staring, with my mouth open.

She took my wrist gingerly. 'Look at you!' she said, more gently. 'Your hands are covered with paint.'

Well, it was true, they were – unlike Mrs

Teerlinc and Nick and the other limners, I had somehow managed to get my fingers as covered with yellow paint as I normally do with ink.

'I'm sorry, mistress,' I stammered. 'I'll wash them at once, but I really don't think I got my gown dirty—'

'No, no,' she said, smiling a little. 'It is not your kirtle I worry about, my dear, it is you. Did you not know some paints are very poisonous? Above all others, the yellow paint made with orpiment. If you eat any at all you could become ill or even die. Never, ever eat or drink while you are painting.'

I was amazed and then thought I'd better curtsy in case she wouldn't let me paint any more. 'I'm sorry; I didn't realize. I won't do it again,' I said.

'Good. Now go to Nick and he will show you how to clean your hands properly.'

I went to the corner of the workroom, where Nick was busy pounding ceruse white again.

'Is it true?' I asked him. 'Are paints poisonous?'

'Most of them are,' he replied. 'Some of

them are quite deadly. It depends what kind. It would amaze you to know the strange things they make paint from. There is a yellow colour I have heard tell of that is made from the urine of cows fed on a special kind of leaf in the Indies.'

That didn't surprise me, knowing Ellie as I do. They sometimes use ten-day-old urine to clean clothes in the laundry. It makes you think twice about wearing your shirts, really it does.

'But that's not poisonous,' I pointed out, 'only nasty.'

'True, but white paint, made with mercury, sends alchemists mad,' said Nick, looking very serious. He waved the pestle to show me the white fragments on the end that he was grinding fine. 'The grinding must be done with great care. And the yellow colour you were using is made with orpiment, which comes from volcanoes and is deadly. It is sometimes used to poison rats for it has no taste or smell.'

Then Nick made his voice sound deep and ghoulish. 'Why, if you accidentally swallowed some of it, you would become sleepy, sick and dizzy. Soon you would be vomiting, with a taste of metal in your mouth and terrible pains in your belly, so you would feel as if you had eaten a rat alive, and it was eating its way out of your stomach—'

'Ugh,' I said, and shuddered.

'And then you would fall into a deathlike sleep and die,' Nick finished, looking triumphant.

After that I paid attention when he showed me how to clean my hands carefully with a rag, and then rinse my fingers with nasty-smelling turpentine and then wash with lye and water until my hands were pink.

It sounds horrible to die of orpiment poisoning. It's a good thing Mrs Teerline was so quick.

Hell's teeth! I have just realized it will soon be dinner time and I must go. The players are still in the courtyard. Richard Fitzgrey is practising standing on his hands – only he isn't at all good at it, and keeps falling over. You'd think all the ladies watching would think less of him for not being able to do something Masou does every day. But no, there they are gasping every time he crashes to the ground, as if he were in danger or something.

Late afternoon, in Carmina her chamber

This is in ink because I have somehow mislaid my graphite pens, Jove blast it. By the way, that's not swearing – I got it from the play we had. I came especially to see how Carmina was faring and perhaps start to divine the mystery of what ails her. As the Queen's most privy Lady Pursuivant, I had best keep in practice, and besides, I hate to see Carmina so sad and tired and weak.

Only I know not how I can investigate anything with such a rabble of girls around! I don't know how they do it; I really don't. We are all here – all six Maids of Honour, that is – and the noise would put a flock of starlings to shame. Nobody has been saying anything with much sense in it at all, and Carmina is presently fast asleep – which is probably just as well because the din would give anyone a relapse.

But perhaps I am being unfair: just as I was writing of the starlings, Mary Shelton started talking to Penelope about diseases.

'It isn't a gaol fever,' she said, 'because there's no fever. And it's not smallpox, because she had that when she was a little girl, and—'

'I do hope she gets better soon,' said Lady Sarah solicitously. 'Her family have had a lot of bad luck recently. Look at what happened to her father at the New Year—'

'What was that?' asked Lady Jane, who isn't very good at remembering gossip that doesn't directly involve her.

'He was hurt in the jousting tournament,' said Mary Shelton patiently. 'Don't you remember? The horse slipped just at the moment when the two were going to meet and—'

'Fell right through the barrier onto the other horse and knocked it down—' put in Penelope excitedly.

'And poor Carmina's father had his leg broken!' finished Lady Sarah.

'It was lucky the bone didn't go through the flesh, for then it would have had to be cut off,' added Mary ghoulishly. 'Once any air touches the bone it rots and you can die.'

'But it didn't,' said Sarah. 'He's at home getting better now.'

'The other one was killed though,' Penelope pointed out. 'It was terribly tragic, because he was in his first ever proper joust, and he just fell off very awkwardly and broke his neck. By the time they took his helmet off, he was dead!'

'Poor Sir John Willoughby was devastated when he was recovered enough to be told,' Sarah remarked, sounding thrilled. 'He said he had rather it was the other way about, him dead and the boy with his leg broken. He swears he will never joust again, even when his leg is mended.'

'It sounds like something that happened to me when I was in France,' put in Lady Jane. 'There was a young nobleman who was desperately in love with me, and I gave him my kerchief as a favour because he was quite handsome and rich. Then he was just show-ing me how his horse could stand on its back legs, when it fell right over onto the nobleman. He broke his leg too. I was so upset.'

Lady Sarah rolled her eyes. 'Serve him right for showing off,' she sniffed. 'Did you laugh?'

'No, of course I didn't!' snapped Lady Jane. 'I was terribly concerned, and I visited his bedside in my best new damask kirtle embroidered with fleurs de lys . . .'

One of the reasons why Lady Jane is so elegant, and gives herself such airs and graces, is because she spent two years at the French Court while her father was an ambassador there. The French Court is the most fashionable in Europe, so of course Lady Jane thinks she knows much more than any of us about Court fashions, which really annoys Lady Sarah, who hasn't been anywhere except England. Of course, the Queen herself has never been abroad either – and doesn't give a fig for the French or any other foreigners.

I am glad poor Carmina is sleeping now, for she has had hardly any peace. I've been here all afternoon keeping her company, and it has been like Cheapside on market day, what with all the coming and going. After I dined in the parlour with the other Maids and Ladies-in-Waiting – but not the Queen, for she was closeted with her papers – Mrs Champernowne made up a tray for Carmina. When she asked if any of us would carry it for her, I offered, as I thought it would give me an excuse to sit with Carmina and perhaps learn more about her mysterious malady.

When I came in, I found Carmina had dribbled a little on the pillowcase in her sleep. So while she was sitting up to try and eat, I got her another one from the chest and put the old one in the pile of laundry by the door.

Just then, she got a cramp in her belly and had to rush to the little garderobe in the corner where the close-stool is. While she was behind the curtain, being sick, Ellie came in to collect the dirty laundry. She peered round the bedpost at the garderobe and dropped a curtsy to Carmina as she came out and climbed back into bed.

'She's pale, in't she?' Ellie hissed at me. 'It's

not the plague, is it?' She made horns with her fingers to ward off bad luck. 'It's too early in the year for that surely?'

'Nobody thinks it is plague!' I scolded Ellie. 'Don't be woodwild. If there was *any* chance of it, the Privy Council would have made the Queen leave immediately and we'd all be locked up in here to die!'

'Not me,' said Ellie. 'Or anyway, I wouldn't die. I've had it. Got it the last time it came and you never get it twice. That was what did for my ma and pa, you know. See? I've still got scars on me neck and me armpits.'

She showed me the ones on her neck, which are about the size of ha'pennies and are where the buboes burst.

'The ones in my armpits are really big,' she said. 'The buboes hurt something terrible until they burst, and then the pus was all stinking and oozing down, but I felt much better . . .'

I didn't really want to hear any more, because I haven't had the plague and it's always frightening to know that there's a sickness you can catch in the morning which could kill you by nightfall.

'My ma and pa didn't get buboes,' Ellie went on, looking sad. 'They might 'ave lived if they did. They just went black all over and died.'

I touched her arm. I didn't really know what to say, because it made me think of my own parents and how sad it was that I couldn't see my mother ever again until Judgement Day. Ellie and I have such different lives, but we are both orphans. Masou is too – his mother died when he was born, and after they came to England his father took sick with the cold and the damp and got consumption and died.

'So anyway,' said Ellie, forcing herself to perk up, 'it ain't plague. So what is it?'

Just then Carmina sighed and put down the chicken tartlet she was nibbling. 'It doesn't even taste good any more,' she said fretfully. 'There's this nasty taste in my mouth all the time. Will you pass me a sweetmeat, Grace? At least they're still nice.'

I passed her some apple leather and she

managed to eat a little before lying back again. She looked tired and sad and a moment later she dozed off.

'Well, nobody else is sickening,' said Ellie with authority. The laundry always knows first when there's an illness going round. 'So maybe it's something she ate.'

'I suppose it could be, though she's hardly eating anything at all,' I replied thoughtfully.

'If it's not that, it's got to be a curse or a spell then,' said Ellie, hefting up the laundry basket and balancing it on her head. 'See you later – hope she don't die.'

No sooner had Ellie left than my uncle, Dr Cavendish, arrived in his furred cramoisie and black brocade gown, followed by Mr Durdon, who is his barber-surgeon. I like Mr Durdon. He is a small, bald, quiet man with stubby fingers, and he always dresses in black cloth so that the blood won't show. He carries his instruments in a leather roll.

Luckily, even though it was after dinner, my Uncle Cavendish was not very drunk and only smelled a little of wine. 'Now, Carmina,' he said kindly, 'I hear you are a little unwell. And as my dear coz is here, we need not wait for Mrs Champernowne.'

Uncle Cavendish sometimes calls me his coz because although he knows perfectly well I am his niece, he doesn't like to think about my mother, whom he misses very much. He never used to drink so much before she died.

He sat down on Carmina's bed, and laid his long hands on her forehead and temples and then her throat and wrists.

'Why do you do that?' I asked curiously, eager to learn all I could in the hope of discovering the cause of Carmina's sickness.

'It is part of the physician's art,' he replied, with his eyes shut and his fingers still on Carmina's wrists. 'There are twelve pulses in the body that teach us of the four humours, and so each must be felt.'

I stayed silent so he could feel them.

'Hmm,' he said at last. 'As Mrs Champernowne says, there is no fever, but your pulses are a little disarranged. Perhaps there is an overplus of melancholy, which would account for the megrim and the vomitus. Have you voided at all?'

This is a physician's way of asking if she had been to the close-stool.

'Yes,' said Carmina. 'It was very nasty smelling.'

'Has it been cleaned? No? Oh, very good.' He went to the garderobe and lifted the curtain to peer into the close-stool. 'Hmm,' he said again, as if it was a very interesting book. 'Well, well.'

He came back and sat next to Carmina once more. 'Now,' he said, 'Mr Durdon?'

Mr Durdon came forward and put a small glass pot on the little table beside Carmina's bed. She looked at it nervously.

'Next time you must answer the call of nature, I desire you to pee into this pot and send it to me immediately,' Uncle Cavendish said, and Carmina nodded. Physicians always scry people's water if they are sick. Sometimes they even taste it! I am so glad women are not allowed to be proper physicians.

'In the meantime, Mr Durdon shall let a

little blood from your left arm, to relieve your body of any excess of the sanguine humour,' my uncle went on.

Carmina frowned unhappily. We all have our blood let at Eastertide, just as the Queen does, to keep us healthy. But nobody likes it, of course.

'A quarter pint only, Mr Durdon,' said my uncle quietly. 'Since she is so pale.'

Mr Durdon nodded and Uncle Cavendish gave place to him. Once he had put the strap on Carmina's bare arm and raised the vein, he opened it very neatly with his little scalpel and let just a quarter pint of her blood into his silver bowl, before stopping it with a cloth and bandaging it. There was not even a spatter on the bedclothes or the rushes. Carmina looked even paler afterwards, I have to say, but I'm sure it will help guard against infection.

'Now,' said my uncle, once Mr Durdon had wiped and packed up his instruments and covered the bowl, 'I want you to stay quiet in bed, Carmina. Eat whatever you have a stomach to, but drink only mild ale or well-watered wine. And we shall see how we go. If you are not better soon, I shall advise the Queen to send a message to your mother for I am sure she will wish to come and nurse you herself.'

Carmina nodded, looking even more worried. 'She's very busy looking after my father and the estate too,' she said anxiously.

Uncle Cavendish patted her hand. 'Of course, of course, we will not trouble her yet, my dear.'

Then he got up, gave me a kiss on the cheek and left the chamber, followed by Mr Durdon, who lifted his hat to me. I sat down again and asked if Carmina wanted me to do anything. I felt very sorry for her, looking so wan after being bled. I did hope she'd say she didn't, so I could write in my daybooke, but alas, she asked me to read her the translation of some of Ovid's pretty tales.

So Carmina's sickness remains a mystery. Usually with illnesses, the patient gets sicker and sicker, till he gets a fever. Then either he starts getting better or he dies. But Carmina has been indisposed for nearly three days now, and before that she was perfectly healthy. She has suffered headaches, sleepiness, lack of appetite – and now belly cramps and a flux.

If only she would eat something more. Mrs Champernowne came in just before all the other Maids arrived, bringing a tisane of comfrey. But Carmina couldn't even drink that, for she said it tasted of metal—

Hell's teeth! I've just had the most horrible thought. Carmina's symptoms – sleepiness, dizziness, a metallic taste in the mouth, then sickness and stomach cramps – are exactly the things Nick Hilliard told me would happen if I ate poisonous orpiment!

I don't know how, but perchance Carmina has swallowed some poison, just like my poor mother did when she drank the poisoned wine meant for the Queen. Only it is slower-acting on Carmina, of course.

God's blood! How awful! But who would want to poison a Maid of Honour? Or could it really have been meant for the Queen?

My heart is pounding so fast I can scarcely

think. I will not mention my suspicion to anyone here. After all, I might be wrong, and besides, if I did, there would be the most tremendous fuss. Sir William Cecil's pursuivants and the Gentlemen of the Guard would be searching the palace and the Court would be thrown into chaos. In all the mayhem, of course, a poisoner could probably slip away.

I simply *must* tell the Queen. But first I think I'll go and talk to Mrs Teerlinc and get a proper account of what happens if you eat a poison like orpiment – just to be sure. Mayhap Nick Hilliard was merely trying to impress me earlier by curdling my blood with his hideous description of the symptoms.

Well, that was exciting! Carmina woke up, blinked a couple of times and then threw up. She did it very neatly, I must say, just like a cat. Luckily, most of it went in the rushes or the pot she was aiming at, and not in the bed. But some of it splattered.

Lady Jane was just leaning over to pat Carmina's hand. She leaped back with a terrible scream and shrieked at Carmina that her kirtle was quite ruined with the spatters. Now Mary Shelton is trying to help Jane with a kerchief dipped in white wine. But Lady Jane is still flapping her hands about and everyone is going, 'Ugh!' at the smell.

'What is all this noise and commotion and rowdiness?'

That was Mrs Champernowne, sweeping in to find Lady Jane in tears over her favourite French kirtle – which has two invisible spots on it – and Lady Sarah giggling because she was well away from the bed and didn't get spattered. Mary is trying to dab the spots on Jane's kirtle, and poor Carmina is bright red with embarrassment and whispering how sorry she is.

'Well, for goodness' sake,' Mrs Champernowne has just snapped. 'There's no need to squeal like stuck pigs. Lady Jane, stand still so Mary can help you. Lady Sarah and Penelope, go and change ready for supper with the Queen – and be sure you do not prattle for she is in a terrible mood, what with the Scots and all. And

Lady Grace, tear yourself away from your scribbling for five seconds, and fetch your uncle back. I will call a Chamberer to sweep up the mess.'

Eventide

I am sitting on the bed, writing away, with my inkpot very carefully stowed on the little shelf in the bedhead which usually holds a watch candle. I have no idea how even more ink stains came upon the bed linen, but I am taking no more chances.

After Carmina was sick, I ran for my Uncle Cavendish and asked him to attend upon her – though I know not how much good he could do, since he had clearly been drinking aqua vitae since he left us.

I escorted him to Carmina's chamber. Then, in order to visit Mrs Teerlinc to confirm my suspicions, I hid my embroidery bag and told Mrs Champernowne I had left it in the workroom.

Mrs Teerlinc is also in charge of the design of the Queen's clothes, and the decorations and wall hangings for the palace, and many other things besides. When I got to the work-room, she was approving sketches for some tapestries that are to be woven in Flanders.

'Now, my Lady Grace,' she said, 'what can I do for you?'

I don't think she was too pleased to see me – she seemed very busy and had a queue of people waiting to consult her.

'Please,' said I, dropping a curtsy to be on the safe side, 'I just wanted to know what really happens if you eat orpiment.'

Her eyebrows went up and I could see she was about to question me. 'Um, only I am worried that, er, one of the Queen's dogs might have eaten some,' I added quickly.

'Well, he will be very sick and sleepy. And he'll have pains in his belly and a great deal of saliva,' Mrs Teerlinc replied.

Carmina had dribbled on her pillow! I swallowed hard. 'Um, might he have a taste of metal in his mouth?'

'Yes,' she said. 'And he might seem dizzy and confused.'

'Oh my goodness!' I gasped, hoping she wouldn't ask how I knew that a dog had a metal taste in his mouth. 'What can I do? Will she . . . I mean, will he die?'

'See if you can get him to eat charcoal, and most certainly prevent him from eating any more of the poison, and then wait. In three days he will be well again – if he has not eaten enough to kill him. How did it happen? Did he find arsenic poison meant for rats?'

'Arsenic has orpiment in it?' I asked quickly.

'Yes, indeed, arsenic is made from orpiment,' said Mrs Teerlinc, turning back to a tailor, who was hopping from leg to leg with impatience. 'Yellow orpiment comes from Mount Etna, where the Italians find it lying about the volcano in lumps. If an alchemist works upon it, then it may be made into a poisonous white powder, arsenic, which they lay as rat bait. Now, my lady, I must attend to my work.'

'Yes, of course,' I said, curtsying like mad. 'Thank you so much.' And I ran out of the room.

So that is confirmed – Nick was not exaggerating at all. Who would have thought that a pretty yellow paint could be so poisonous? And Mrs Teerlinc's description of the symptoms certainly sounds like Carmina's mysterious illness. But how on earth is Carmina getting arsenic? She could not be eating it by accident, for she has not been up to the workroom at all – it would make more sense if *I* was sickening. Carmina isn't really eating anything at all.

It seems I have stumbled upon a riddle that is quite definitely – and most unexpectedly – a matter for Her Majesty's Lady Pursuivant. I must tell the Queen. I'll try and speak to her after supper.

Last thing at night

Her Majesty is such a wonderful person. She supped late with my Lord of Leicester, her Captain of the Guard Mr Hatton and two of the Ladies-in-Waiting. Then she was going to play cards to distract her mind from all the foreign problems, but I simply had to talk to her. I spoke to the Gentleman of the Guard who was at the door to her Withdrawing Chamber, and said that Her Majesty had particularly ordered me to give her an account of Carmina, so she could decide whether to send for Carmina's mother.

It took me ages to persuade him, but at last he sighed and said he would enquire.

I heard him speak softly to the Queen.

'Hm? News of Carmina?' she replied. 'Oh, is it my Lady Grace Cavendish? Yes, I shall see her.'

So the gentleman held the door for me. I went in and curtsied to Mr Hatton and my Lord of Leicester, who scowled down his nose at me for interrupting his private evening with the Queen. He is famously proud, and everyone hates him because he is still the Queen's favourite. I don't mind him being haughty with me, because I know that he truly cares about the Queen. Mr Hatton is nicer but not at all interested in Maids of Honour, or in

Ladies-in-Waiting; nor is he seemingly inclined to marry, although he is a famously good dancer and very elegant and witty.

I went to the Queen and sank to me knees before her. She gave me her hand to get up again and I whispered, 'Your Majesty, I must speak to you privily.'

She raised her eyebrows and gave me one of those looks that make me feel she can see right through me and out the other side. Just for a moment she hesitated, looking at her cards, which were face down. She was playing Primero and there was quite a big pot of money in the middle of the table. 'What is it about?' she asked.

'Carmina, Your Majesty, but it must be private,' I replied.

She stood with a rustle of silk, frowning slightly, and of course everyone else stood too. We went off to her Privy Chamber, which was empty just then.

'Now, Grace, I hope you are not troubling me with anything trivial or scandalous?' the Queen said warningly.

'Oh, no, Your Majesty,' I told her. 'I would never do that. This is a matter of great importance — only I may be mistaken, so I would speak with you privately.'

Her eyes narrowed. 'Well?'

'You know Carmina's sickness?'

She nodded a little impatiently.

I took a deep breath. 'Well, I don't think she is naturally sick. I think she might have eaten poison — perhaps arsenic.' And as quickly as I could I described the symptoms of arsenic poisoning, and told her that Carmina's symptoms were exactly the same.

'Why would anyone want to poison Carmina?' demanded the Queen dubiously, when I had finished.

'I do not know, Your Majesty,' I replied. 'I cannot think of a reason. Perchance it has happened accidentally, though I do not know how that could occur . . .' I trailed off because the whole idea was so upsetting.

The Queen was frowning and thinking hard. 'Who else have you spoken to of this?' she asked.

'No one, Your Majesty. I knew what a fuss there would be if poison was suspected.'

'Then how did you ask Mrs Teerlinc about it?' the Queen wanted to know.

'I said I thought one of the dogs might have eaten rat poison,' I explained.

Her Majesty smiled. 'And one of them might, as well,' she said, nodding. 'Well done, Grace. As usual I am delighted by your discretion. You did right to speak to me alone and first. I doubt it could be a deliberate poisoning, and yet it is hard to see how it could occur by chance. Will you make enquiries for me, as my privy Lady Pursuivant? Continuing to be very discreet?'

'Of course, Your Majesty,' I murmured, curtsying and feeling very proud. 'Your Majesty does me great honour.'

'But no mad escapades, Grace,' she added. 'Come to me with anything you find. Simply say that you have news of Carmina and I will see you whenever you wish, since I know I can trust you not to din my ears with begging for offices and pensions.'

I felt even more proud. Most of the time it

is difficult to speak directly with the Queen, because she is always very busy. 'Your Majesty, is there anything we can do to protect Carmina, even without knowing the source of the poison?' I asked anxiously.

'Certainly there is,' the Queen replied. 'I will take measures to do so, and to foil any poisoner's attempts to harm me. Do not be alarmed by anything you may hear about me: I think my stomach is about to become very delicate.' And she smiled and winked.

I kissed her hand and we went back to the Withdrawing Chamber – where I thought both Mr Hatton and my Lord of Leicester looked suspiciously innocent. Neither of them is above cheating to make sure they lose to the Queen – who, as they both know, very much likes to win.

The Gentleman of the Guard showed me out. I came back to our bedchamber to find Lady Sarah arguing with Mary Shelton on the subject of another remedy for spots. Mary says that Sarah should use diluted aqua vitae to remove her face paint completely, and then rinse with rose water. Sarah insists that a decoction of nettle leaves, followed by ashes of honeybees in goose fat, is much better. *I* think that if Sarah laid off face paint completely, she would not have half so many spots, but she won't listen to me.

So now I am on the trail of a mysterious poisoner, though I know not where to look first. And I wonder how I can get Carmina to eat charcoal . . .

Mid-morning

I have had a very busy morning so far, and this is the first time I have had a moment in my chamber to sit and write. I only had time to nibble my bread and small beer at break-fast, before I was sent on an errand for Mrs Champernowne. I was to fetch kerchiefs from the laundry for Carmina — which was lucky, because it meant I could ask Ellie to help me with my investigation.

Ellie came with me to Carmina's chamber. I carried the kerchiefs, while she carried a huge basket of bedclothes balanced on her head. She says it is much less hard on her back that way.

We had to go through the Outer Courtyard, where the players were rehearsing a scene full of falling over and rolling. Masou was on the other side of the courtyard where the players could all see him, standing on his hands and practising juggling with his bare feet. His face was very funny because it showed such a mixture of sulkiness and concentration. I think he was trying to impress the players with how well he can stand on his hands – unlike Richard Fitzgrey.

Ellie and I stayed to watch, where no one would see us, behind one of the very elaborate buttresses for the chapel.

'So, now,' said Ellie, putting the basket down and sitting on it, just as Masou walked over on his hands to join us, still juggling. 'I know that expression, my lady. What are you up to?' she demanded.

I swore both Ellie and Masou to secrecy, and then I told them about Carmina and how I suspected that she might have eaten poison.

Ellie narrowed her eyes. 'Cor,' she said enthusiastically. 'It'll be them Scots, trying to poison our Queen. It's just the sort of thing they'd do. Everyone knows they're always killing their own kings and queens, and rebelling and suchlike. It's shocking.'

'Perhaps,' I said doubtfully. 'But why would the Scots aim at the Queen and get Carmina instead? If it was in our food, we'd all be ill. I think it must be someone who wants only to poison Carmina. But who could that be?'

'One of them wicked Scots, *practising* for poisoning the Queen,' said Ellie darkly.

'An evil djinn released by a powerful enemy of hers,' suggested Masou, stopping juggling because he was interested now.

'I don't know,' I said. 'I'm not sure Carmina has got any enemies.' But then I remembered something Lady Jane had said. 'Lady Jane mentioned Carmina's recent inheritance,' I muttered to myself. 'Maybe somebody else wants it and stands to inherit if Carmina dies! I must talk to Lady Sarah as soon as I can and see if she knows who Carmina's property would go to. And Ellie,' I went on quickly. 'Could you find out tactfully which of the kitchens makes the food for the Maids of Honour? And see if there's anyone new or suspicious – or with a grudge against Carmina – who might be poisoning her food,' I finished.

Ellie nodded.

'How long has Carmina been unwell?' Masou asked.

'About three days,' I told him.

'Aha!' shouted Masou. 'Of course! It's the pig-eating players. They've been here four days – first in the village and now pestering the Court – and you say that your friend first took sick three days ago. So that's proof!'

I do not think it is proof, though it is certainly interesting.

Masou was now scowling at the players across the courtyard. 'Maybe that Greyfitz thinks—'

'Fitzgrey,' corrected Ellie.

'Ptui! Fitzgrey, then. Maybe he thinks Carmina's inheritance should be his,' Masou suggested.

I'd never heard such nonsense. 'Why on earth would he? He's not related to her in any way,' I pointed out.

'Mayhap the true villain paid him,' Masou pressed, refusing to give up, 'or enchanted him, or—'

'Anyway, how could he do it?' I demanded. 'He's not allowed anywhere near Carmina – or the kitchens.'

Masou shrugged. 'Isn't he supposed to be an actor? Maybe he disguised himself as a rat-catcher.'

'Hmph,' sniffed Ellie. 'I'm sure someone as kind as Mr Fitzgrey would never—'

'Kind?' I interrupted Ellie.

'*Mr* Fitzgrey?' sneered Masou.

Ellie went pink. 'Well, he wanted bread and cheese fetching from the Hall Kitchens, so I went and got them for 'im, di'n't I?' she muttered. 'Very polite he was too, *and* he gave me a groat for my trouble.'

Masou scowled and looked even more put out. 'You never fetch bread and cheese for me!' he accused Ellie.

'Why should I? You can go to the buttery for yourself,' snapped Ellie. 'You wouldn't give me a groat, neither.'

'Why should I?' began Masou hotly.

'Stop it, both of you!' I said. 'None of the players is being poisoned—'

'More's the pity,' muttered Masou.

'– or I'd know *exactly* where to look,' I told him severely. 'I can't believe you're being so jealous. They'll be gone at the end of the week.'

'Hmph,' said Masou, starting to juggle again.

It occurred to me that the poisoner had to be getting the poison from somewhere. The painters' workroom was one possibility – I knew there was orpiment there – but the rat-catcher was another.

'I really need you to ask about the rat-catcher for me, Masou,' I said. 'Find out if he's been called in recently, or if anyone knows him well. I can't do it because I can't talk to the right people.'

'All right,' grunted Masou, still juggling as he wandered off to annoy the players with more tumbling tricks.

Ellie and I took the kerchiefs and the clean bed linen up to Carmina's chamber. Then Ellie hurried back to the laundry while I went in search of Lady Sarah, who is the best source of gossip I know.

I first tried our bedchamber, which turned

out to be empty. So here I am seizing the opportunity to write up my daybooke. But now that is done, so I shall stop writing and continue my search for Sarah. I am hopeful that she will be able to tell me all about Carmina's possible heirs.

Later, after dinner, in Carmina her chamber

I found Lady Sarah sitting on a bench in the Outer Courtyard with Penelope. They were both working on their embroidery and said they needed the bright daylight to see clearly by. Coincidentally, the players were rehearsing their lines nearby, and I noticed that Sarah's eyes were more often on Richard Fitzgrey than on her embroidery.

'And how is Carmina today?' Sarah asked, knowing that I had been to her chamber. 'Mrs Champernowne wouldn't let me go and see her this morning, even though I needed to borrow some of her rouge. Apparently, she needs to rest.'

'She was sick many times in the night, poor dear,' Penelope said. 'I think she must be very tired.'

'Yes, she was sleeping when I saw her,' I agreed. And then I saw the perfect opportunity to find out what I needed to know. 'Poor thing, and she was so pleased about her inheritance,' I remarked. 'I wonder who it came from?'

'Oh, from a great-aunt nobody liked very much, except Carmina,' declared Sarah authoritatively. 'She was famously mean and strict but was fond of Carmina when she was a little girl.'

'How do you know?' I asked, a little breathless because my plan was working so brilliantly.

'My mother is friends with her mother because they were at Court together in the train of Queen Catherine, way back under King Henry,' explained Sarah with a toss of her head.

'So who gets the inheritance if Carmina should die?' I asked, then thought that that was a bit bald and tactless and I didn't want to start any more wild rumours. So I added, 'I mean, I'm sure she won't, but—'

'I think it would all go to her cousin Frederick Bates,' said Sarah. 'At least, I think he's a cousin, though he's quite a distant one.'

I tried not to show my excitement; maybe this Frederick was the villainous poisoner! 'Have I seen him?' I asked. 'Is he here at Court?'

'No, he's in the Netherlands at the moment, I think,' replied Sarah, wrinkling her brow in an effort to remember. 'I've only met him once myself, ages ago, when he was a boy. And he was the dullest boy you can imagine.' She sighed as she caught Richard Fitzgrey rehearsing a duel. 'Not like Richard Fitzgrey.'

'You mean the *player*?' asked Lady Jane, who had just arrived.

Lady Sarah gave her a very annoyed look as she sat down on the other side of Penelope. At that moment Penelope remembered she had a music lesson so she hurried away, leaving Lady Sarah and Lady Jane sitting next to each other. I decided to back off and watch the fun from a safe distance. If they had been cats, their fur would have been standing up and their tails bottled. Both ladies were edging their bums towards the end of the bench nearest the players, while pretending that they weren't, of course.

'Tut,' said Lady Jane. 'I fear me that if you sit in the sunlight so much, dear Sarah, you will find even more freckles fighting the spots on your nose. Prithee, move here where 'tis more shady.'

'You are so kind, sweet Jane,' sneered Lady Sarah, staying exactly where she was. 'But are you not afrighted that the sunlight will make your hair even drier? I understand that bleached hair is *so* delicate.'

'How considerate!' trilled Lady Jane. 'Of course, you would know far more than me about coloured hair, Sarah.'

'About most things, I should think,' snapped Sarah. 'Except, of course, Frenchmen . . .'

And they glared at each other, looking quite ready to scratch each other's eyes out.

'What in Heaven's name are you two doing here?' Mrs Champernowne came bustling up behind the bench. 'Do you not know better than to sit in full sunlight without your hats?

Get away with you now! Go and sit in the shade.'

'I was just warning Lady Sarah about it,' sniffed Lady Jane.

'Then follow your own advice,' snapped Mrs Champernowne, and frowned until both of them stood up and huffed off in different directions. Then she sat herself down on the bench at the end nearest the players, despite all that dangerous sunlight, took out her blackwork and started humming.

Luckily she hadn't spotted me, and I quietly moved further away, behind a piece of castle scenery. I didn't want her to notice I had no hat either.

Behind the scenery, I came upon the oldest of the players, who was making a big yellow sun on a piece of canvas, with the pot of yellow paint beside him. I wondered if it was the poisonous orpiment yellow, or perhaps the yellow made of cow's pee. Perhaps this could be the source of the poison affecting Carmina! I decided I would ask Nick Hilliard and Mrs Teerlinc about it next time I was in the workroom.

For now, I was intending to visit Carmina and learn all I could about her cousin, Frederick, but first I wanted to find some charcoal. After hearing Mrs Teerlinc's advice, I was determined to persuade Carmina to eat a little, in the hope that it would help her feel better.

Besides, I thought, if Carmina got better after eating it, it would prove that she *was* being poisoned with arsenic.

I headed for Lady Horsley's confectionery kitchen in the hopes of taking a few bits of charcoal out of the sack she has there. Most ladies can distil strong flower waters and make comfits, but Lady Horsley is quite famous for her skills. She sometimes makes subtleties of marchpane for the Queen's own banquet, though of course there is a Royal Confectioner as well.

The Queen has given her leave to use the old stillroom that was the Court Confectioner's in King Harry's time. I love it, for it is a high-ceilinged room, with narrow shelves up one wall for drying the sweetmeats. There is no great fireplace like in a proper kitchen, just a row of small grills over charcoal fires, many chafing dishes and a supply of best charcoal.

When I arrived, the windows were all open to let the fumes out. But where was that supply of best charcoal? I had hoped I would see a sack of it somewhere, waiting for me to borrow a few lumps. But no, there was no sign of it. Perhaps it was stored in one of the cupboards.

Lady Horsley was wearing a plain white cap and apron over an old velvet gown. Her thin, pale face was quite pink with stirring an earthenware pot on a chafing dish full of hot charcoal. I knew at once what she was making – you can't mistake that wonderful smell of oranges from Spain – it was marmelada sweet-meats, one of my favourite treats. On the shelves there were wafers, and sweet chestnuts soaking in sugar syrup, and apricots and plums waiting for their frosty white sugar coats to harden. Lady Seymour, Lady Horsley's friend, was mixing a big bowl of pounded sugar loaf – just the *white* sugar, not the sticky *brown* sugar from the pointed end of the loaf – and Mary Shelton had just arrived as well.

'Mary, my dear, how is poor Carmina?' asked Lady Horsley in her kind, soft voice.

'Not well,' said Mary Shelton, shaking her head. 'She says her stomach is sore and she won't eat anything but sweetmeats. Everyone has been so kind – she has had kissing comfits from Mrs Champernowne, and sugared violets and marchpanes from Lady Sarah, and even some Turkey sweetmeats. Olwen is making her sweet wafers on a wafer-iron too.'

'Do you like sweetmeats, Grace?' asked Lady Horsley, stirring the marmelada mixture briskly.

'Oh, yes,' I said. 'Sugar is my favourite spice of all. I like the sugar ribbons – and marmeladas, of course.'

'I am making some more ribbons,' put in Lady Seymour. 'See, there's the gumdragon soaking, ready to bind the sugar together. Here, have one from yesterday.' She handed me a long ribbon in the shape of a bow, from one of the drying shelves. It was coloured yellow and blue to look like marble, and it was quite beautiful. When they make sugar goblets and plates for banquets, I can never decide whether to eat them or keep them to look at.

I crunched up some of the ribbon.

'Have the broken ones,' said Lady Horsley, giving Mary and me two big handfuls. 'I dropped a whole tray this morning.'

I put them in my petticoat pocket to give to Ellie later.

'Would you fetch me some nibbed almonds, my dear?' Lady Horsley asked. She was talking to Mary Shelton, but I pretended I thought it was me, so I could have an excuse to open all the cupboards and look for charcoal.

I found big sugar loaves waiting to be broken up and pounded, jars of almonds and gumdragon and eggs, and even more jars of orange flower water and rose water, but no charcoal! I pretended I hadn't seen the almonds and kept opening cupboards.

I spotted a little oven in one corner, with a separate cupboard next to it. I hastened over and opened the door. Yes! There was the charcoal in a big sack.

'Lady Grace, what are you doing?' asked

Lady Horsley, sounding puzzled. By this time, I noticed, Mary Shelton was being helpful and had found the nibbed almonds in the first cupboard I'd opened.

'I, er . . . Oooh!' I gasped. 'I thought I saw a mouse run in here!' Well, it was the best excuse I could think of at such short notice. 'Look! There it is!' I cried, pulling on the sack of charcoal so that it fell over and scattered little pieces of charcoal across the floor.

Lady Horsley sighed and smiled. 'Lord save us, Grace, you are as clumsy as Mrs Champernowne says you are – which I didn't think possible! We'll put Grimalkin in here tonight to catch the mouse.'

I swept up the charcoal and managed to grab a few pieces, lift my kirtle and slip them into my petticoat pocket. I had to be terribly careful not to get any more black dust on my kirtle – I'd already got a bit dirty when the sack fell over. Now there's charcoal smeared on my petticoat too. I hope it comes out more easily than ink.

Lady Horsley offered Mary Shelton and me

some more sweetmeats, and then handed Mary a whole tray of them.

'Would you take these sweetmeats up to Carmina, without nibbling any, and tell her I shall be there myself to read to her shortly?' she asked.

Mary nodded, took the bowl and left.

I was just about to go with her, when Lady Horsley decided that the marmelada – which was a stiff paste now, and coming away from the sides of the dish – was ready to come off the heat.

'Would you be so good as to cover these with waxed paper for me, Lady Grace?' she asked, as she scooped the mixture into the metal moulds and pressed it down.

I hurried to help. The marmeladas won't be ready until they have dried for a month, but then – yum!

When we had finished, Lady Horsley chivvied me out of the stillroom, with her friend Lady Seymour, and then locked it carefully. I suppose if it wasn't locked, none of the sweetmeats would last out the night, but I sighed, for how was I supposed to get any more charcoal?

I had to wait until after dinner before I could go and see Carmina. We ate with the Queen in the Privy Parlour. She seemed to be in a terrible temper, and kept sending away food on the grounds that it was not cooked properly – or had been burned – until finally two gentlemen were sent to buy pasties for all of us from the cookshop in the nearest village. I thought it was very cleverly done – nobody would have guessed Her Majesty was worried about poison at all.

Mrs Champernowne had made a posset of ale for Carmina, so I volunteered to take it up. At last I thought I would have a chance to talk to her privately about the mysterious Frederick, and give her the charcoal in my petticoat pocket. The only trouble was, the idea of me carrying a jug of ale posset up the stairs made Mrs Champernowne so nervous that she insisted on coming with me! She watched, eagle-eyed, as I poured it out, though I didn't spill a drop.

Carmina managed to drink a little. She

looked very pale, poor dear, and was bored and weary, but she said she felt better.

At last Mrs Champernowne took herself off and I settled down with my embroidery work, watching in case Carmina was going to be sick – with my luck it would go all over my new white kirtle and everybody would blame me. I started stitching butterflies in silk – it's to be a stomacher for the Queen one day.

'You're very kind to keep me company, Grace,' said Carmina anxiously. 'Are you sure you wouldn't like to go and watch the players rehearse with the others?'

'Not at all,' I replied. 'I don't know what they think they're up to. They're acting as bad as gentlemen laying suit to Lady Sarah, I think.'

Carmina giggled. 'I've missed so much,' she said. 'You've no idea how boring it is here. Lady Horsley came and read to me earlier, but she sounds as if she's a vicar the way she drones on.'

So I told her about Lady Jane and Lady Sarah arguing over who could sit nearest the players, and then about Mrs Champernowne shooing them away and sitting there herself. Carmina laughed at that.

'Oh, and by the way,' I added casually, as I got the bits of charcoal out of my petticoat pocket, which was now all black, 'I've heard that this strengthens the stomach and you should eat it.'

'What is it?' asked Carmina suspiciously.

'It's, um, it's just charcoal, and it makes your—'

'Ugh, no, I'm not eating that! You must be Bedlam, Grace — it's disgusting.'

'You put pounded ashes of mouse tail in goose fat on your nose last week,' I accused her. 'Why isn't that disgusting?'

'That was because I had a spot and Sarah said it would help,' declared Carmina.

'It doesn't do anything for *her* spots,' I pointed out.

'How do you know? She might have even more if she didn't put medicines and creams on them,' Carmina argued.

'I don't see how,' I muttered. 'Come on,' I said, coaxing. 'Just try a little charcoal . . .'

She made a wry face and pushed my hand away. 'I'm sorry, Grace, I can't eat anything at all at the moment – not even Lady Horsley's lovely sugared apricots.'

Well, I wasn't going to give up that easily, so when she wasn't looking I put some bits of charcoal on the apricots in the bowl. I hoped she might eat some without noticing and that they might help defeat the poison. Then I offered her the rest of the posset.

She looked at it and sighed. 'I'm just not hungry. My mother sent me some cakes yesterday – French bisket bread with gold leaf – and I couldn't eat more than one of them either.'

'I've heard you have an admirer overseas who's been sending you things too,' I hinted mysteriously. It was the only way I could think of broaching the subject of Frederick without letting her know of my suspicions.

'Oh?' said Carmina with interest. 'Who?'

Hell's teeth! That's not what she was supposed to say. I was hoping she might blush and ask how I knew. 'Um, I just heard,' I replied vaguely.

'No,' said Carmina. 'Everyone's been very

kind, bringing me possets and custards and sweetmeats and such, but I've had nothing from overseas.'

'Oh, I must have heard wrong,' I said airily. 'You know what it's like here, everyone gossips all the time and nobody really knows what they're talking about. I expect you don't even *have* a cousin in the Netherlands, do you?'

'Well, yes, actually I do,' Carmina responded. 'Cousin Frederick.' She went ever so slightly pink and looked down at her sheets. 'When Great-aunt Catherine made her will, there was talk of us marrying – we're not close cousins, you see. I think she left me the manor of Chigley hoping it would come to us both if the match went ahead. But then Frederick left for the Netherlands.'

'He must have been most put out to miss out on the inheritance,' I suggested, hoping Carmina would confirm my suspicions.

'Oh, no, I don't think so,' she declared. 'He recently wed some incredibly rich Flemish merchant's daughter. So he's simply rolling in money now.'

'Oh,' I said lamely. 'I thought he was very poor and that's why he went overseas.'

'He was quite poor. He's a younger son so he got nothing much from his father. But he's been doing really well as a merchant at the Antwerp exchange – something boring to do with wool contracts – and now he's married the Flemish girl he could probably buy my father's demesne several times over.' She giggled. 'My mother is very cross about it – she wishes she had pushed harder for the match now.'

'Are you sad he married someone else?' I asked solicitously.

Carmina laughed again. 'Lord above, no, he's the most boring person you could ever meet and I hear he's got quite fat. They do in the Netherlands, you know – it's the pancakes and cherry beer for breakfast.'

'Oh!' I tried to laugh with her, but really I was quite disappointed. Frederick had seemed such a perfect solution to the problem of who could want to poison Carmina, and now it seemed he was too rich to care much about her little manor of Chigley.

'I so hope I'll be well enough to watch the comedy,' she said, after a pause while she watched me sew. 'I thought Richard Fitzgrey was wonderful in the tragedy, even though the story upset me – besides the ending being sad anyway.'

'Why would it upset you?' I asked.

'Feuds are horrible things, not romantic at all,' Carmina explained. 'They make people behave quite stupidly and they drag on and on and on.'

'How do you know?'

'My family had a feud with the Harringtons for about a hundred years. It started over a sheep, I think. Or was it a cow?'

'Oh!' I was surprised and excited. This could be another lead. 'I thought only foreigners had feuds.'

'It was back in the reign of the Sixth King Henry,' Carmina went on. 'We were Lancaster men and they were York followers. When the Yorkists deposed poor King Henry, old Lord Harrington came and stole some livestock and wouldn't give it back. And then one of my great-uncles got killed trying to get the sheep, or cows, or whatever, back by stealth. And then there was a big riot and the Harrington village got burned. And then, well, I don't know quite how it went, but at last the Lord Protector in young King Edward's reign forced my father and Lord Harrington to make it up. They had to swear never to fight again, which I think they were quite glad to do on the whole and so the feud was composed and that was that.'

'Is it really finished and done with?' I pressed, unwilling to abandon this new source of potential suspects.

'Oh, yes,' insisted Carmina. 'Nobody would dare fight a feud now. The Queen would send an army, like they do in Scotland, and hang everybody!'

So that was all I discovered on the subjects of Frederick and the Harringtons, and I was left with no potential poisoners at all! Though it was interesting to hear about a real live feud — just like the Italians and the Scots have — even if it was over nearly twenty years ago.

Then Carmina said she was feeling very

thirsty and would I mind going and finding a Chamberer to fetch some mild ale for her. So I went out and down the passage, where I found that very annoying young page Robin, who is the little brother of one of the Ladies-in-Waiting. He was talking to the old man I had seen painting in the courtyard.

'Now then, lad,' the man was saying. 'Are you page to the Maids of Honour?'

'Yes, I am,' said Robin brightly, though it wasn't true. He runs errands for us sometimes when he isn't playing football with the dog-pages.

'I have another little gift here for one of them, the one that's called Mistress Carmina Willoughby,' the old player said, holding a package out nervously in both hands. 'Would you give it her with this note?'

'What's it worth?' Robin asked shamelessly.

The old man didn't mind. 'Nothing but a farthing,' he said firmly, 'for it's nothing scandalous, only from one as knew her when she was a little 'un and wishes to be remembered to her.'

'Well enough then,' said Robin, holding his hand out for the package and the coin.

The old man gave both to him. 'Thanking you kindly, young master,' he said, and went back down the passageway where the Gentleman of the Guard was waiting for him.

Robin was fingering the small package consideringly, when I swooped down on him from behind.

'What's that then, Robin?' I asked.

He jumped and looked guilty as he had been peeping inside the wrapping. 'Sweetmeats for Carmina,' he said.

'I'll give them to her,' I told him, and held my hand out.

Robin hesitated a moment and then shrugged. 'Is it true she's sick to death with leprosy and like to die?' he asked ghoulishly as he handed over the sweetmeats.

'Yes,' I told him, 'so you'd best run away quick before your nose drops off.' Which he did, with his hand held carefully over his nose.

I looked at the package in my hand, now full of suspicion at the old player. As Masou had pointed out, the players came a few days ago, which is when Carmina first started to get sick. And now here was one far too old to be even the most hopeless admirer – sending her sweetmeats as a present. *And* he had been painting that yellow sun on the scenery earlier, so he probably had access to poisonous orpiment as well!

At last it was all beginning to fit together. The old player arrived with the others, and then Carmina became ill. If I could find out whether he had sent her sweetmeats before, and why he might wish her ill, then that would make it certain.

I examined the package again. It was wrapped in a piece of fine linen, with a note tied to it by a ribbon. I decided I would ask Carmina if she remembered the old man before I delivered his present.

After I had found a Chamberer and asked her to get some ale from the buttery, I went back to Carmina and sat down next to her.

'There was a funny thing,' I said casually, giving her just the note. 'The oldest player was asking after you. He said he knew you when you were a child and wanted to be remembered to you. Do you know him?'

Carmina frowned and sighed. 'Yes, I do. His name is Sampson Childs, and he used to be my father's clerk years ago,' she explained. 'He got into terrible trouble with my father over a girl in the village. He refused to marry her and left with a band of players that came one Christmas. Now he's here with Mr Alleyn's company. A few days ago, when they arrived, he gave me kissing comfits – delicious sugared violets and rose leaves – with a letter begging my father to take him back. You see, he has lumbago now and finds it hard to travel about with the players.'

I could hardly breathe at this, I was so excited. The old player had given Carmina sweetmeats *before* she fell sick. It was beginning to look as if I had found the poisoner! 'Do you think your father *would* take him back?' I asked.

Carmina shook her head. 'I don't really think so. Father had to give the girl a dowry so she could marry somebody else, and it was quite expensive.'

Aha! I thought. All is starting to make sense. Perhaps this Sampson Childs is pursuing a feud for being dismissed from Mr Willoughby's household!

So I didn't say anything at all about the packet of sweetmeats he had sent Carmina. I mean to investigate them thoroughly and prove whether they are really poisoned. I am certain that they are!

Carmina has dozed off now and I can think of no more to write for the moment, so I shall continue my investigations at once.

Later

Jove blast it! That was disappointing. And I must scribble quickly, for I am in my chamber, supposed to be changing my raiment again – this time for supper.

I went to find Masou and Ellie to enquire

whether they had learned anything about the kitchens of the rat-catcher. They were in the den in the coppice again, and Masou was looking a little less sulky this time.

'We are to help the players with their comedy,' he explained. 'So we will not have to sit and watch those idiots prancing around thinking that they are princes and pashas.'

Ellie snickered. 'I never heard the like,' she said. 'You're just jealous, isn't he, Grace?'

'Yes, but I don't know why,' I sniffed. 'You're not in love with any of the Maids of Honour, Masou, so you needn't mind if they make idiots of themselves over a player. Unless you're really after Mrs Champernowne . . .'

That made Ellie giggle, but Masou looked extremely haughty. 'When the time comes for me to wed,' he told us with great dignity, 'I shall take a ship painted in red and gold with silken sails. It shall be full of great warriors, and together we shall sail southwards to the land of the Barbary Corsairs, where we will cannonade and raid them until their Bey surrenders to me. And then I shall marry his daughters.'

'His *daughters*!' hooted Ellie. 'You have to choose, you know. You can't have all of them.'

'I can,' said Masou. 'I am a Mussulman and I may have four wives if I am rich enough.' He was juggling twigs and stones. 'Which I shall be,' he added.

'Cor,' said Ellie very dubiously. 'The way Cook Parsons talks he reckons one wife is too many – seeing she's always on at him to feed every one of her greedy relations from the kitchen stores.'

That finally reminded me of why I was there. 'Did you hear anything in the kitchens?' I asked.

'Well,' said Ellie, 'I went to all four of them – the Hall Kitchen, the Great Kitchen, the Lesser Kitchen and the Queen's Privy Kitchen – and they've none of them got new staff or new purveyors. And nobody that works there has took sick from any of the Court's food – which they would have if it was poisoned because most of 'em are eating the Court's food all the time, along with their families, cousins, friends and neighbours! It's a scandal – worse than what happens with the laundry soap – but there's nobody suspicious nor nothing!'

I nodded, not too disappointed because I hadn't really expected anything else. If you wanted to poison just one person, you could not do it through the kitchens, because we all share the dishes out among us and we would all get sick and die.

'You know,' I said, 'the Queen has certainly ordered special food for Carmina now. Do you think you could find out who's preparing it?'

'Course!' Ellie grinned mischievously. 'If they'll let me in again.' And she pulled a big lump of bacon and egg pie out of her pocket and offered me some. I hadn't the heart to take it from her since she so rarely has any spare food to offer, but Masou did. Since he is a Mussulman, he's not supposed to eat pork, but I don't know why not, and he often does anyway.

'What about the rat-catcher?' I asked Masou.

Masou shrugged and answered with his mouth full. 'He put down poison against the rats before the Queen came, but he's not allowed to do it when she is in residence in case one of her dogs eats the bait and dies. So recently he's been using terriers and traps instead. He said I could come and watch the next ratting contest if I liked. But I think I will not, for I take no sport in seeing such things as a dog killing live rats. He said some of the young gents bet whole manors on it when they can't go to the cockpit at Westminster.'

I shook my head. I really hate it when animals are made to fight so people can bet on them; it doesn't seem fair. All the young gentlemen love things like that and talk endlessly about the latest cockfighting champion – and even the Queen enjoys the bearbaiting – but I always say I have a megrim so I don't have to go and watch. I was pleased Masou didn't like ratting.

Then I remembered the package of sweetmeats from Sampson Childs. Since the poisoner couldn't be working through the kitchens, sending sweetmeats seemed an ideal way to poison Carmina. I took it out carefully and opened it. Inside was a little wooden box with a very expensive kind of sweetmeat from Turkey – a kind of pink jelly, embellished with gold leaf and fine-pounded sugar. Ellie was eager to try it, but I explained where it had come from and told her and Masou of my suspicions.

'Where is the rat-catcher now?' I asked Masou.

'Down by the New Buildings at the bottom of the orchard,' Masou replied, gallantly letting Ellie have the best bit of pie with the egg in it, since after all she had filched it. 'You know, the ones Good King Edward built near the palace.'

'Yes. Could we go and see him, do you think?' I asked. 'We must test these sweetmeats to see whether they are poisoned.'

Ellie frowned. 'I'd have to come with you, my lady,' she said, 'and save your reputation what would be in tatters by now, if it weren't for me.'

So we all went and found the rat-catcher, who was sitting in the little yard by one of the rows of rickety new buildings, eating bread and cheese. He stood up hastily when he saw me and took off his cap and bowed.

'My lady desires to see a rat,' said Masou, with his nose in the air, as if he was a pasha himself.

I smiled when the rat-catcher looked from Masou to me and back in bewilderment. 'I am not afeared of them,' I explained. 'Only I have an experiment I want to try.'

Masou gave the rat-catcher the sixpence I had given him for the purpose, and the rat-catcher grunted and went inside the house. He returned with a wooden cage containing a young grey rat.

'My lady don't believe rats will eat everything,' put in Ellie.

'Oh they will, my lady,' said the rat-catcher. 'They'd eat you, if they could.' He grinned and I think he was expecting me to say, 'Eek!' and 'Ugh!' but I was too busy feeling guilty about offering the poor rat in the cage something that might well kill it.

Ellie caught me looking anxiously at the poor thing. 'I know,' she whispered. 'Why don't we try it on that old cow Mrs Fadget instead?'

I laughed. Mrs Fadget is the Deputy

Laundress and Ellie hates her. But I had to find out if Sampson Childs was really trying to poison Carmina, so I took out a little square of pink jelly and pushed it through the bars.

The rat sniffed it suspiciously, nibbled it even more suspiciously, and then seemed to get very excited. I was feeling peculiar – all tense and sorry for the rat, as well as hopeful that it would show me I had found the poisoner.

Well, the rat sat up with its whiskers twitching and started nibbling through the sweetmeat very quickly indeed, as if it thought we might change our minds about giving it something so lovely and take it back.

We watched for a while, but the rat simply finished the jelly square and looked around hopefully for more. Then it went and drank some water and washed its paws very neatly.

I couldn't help it. I said, 'Ahh!' at the sight of the little animal washing its paws. Both Ellie and Masou looked at me as if I were mad.

'There, my lady,' said the rat-catcher. 'See? They'll eat anything, they will.'

'I suppose that's why it's possible to poison

them,' I said thoughtfully. I was trying to find a way of asking the rat-catcher how long it might take a poisoned rat to die, without letting him know that I was actually testing the sweet-meats for poison. I didn't want him gossiping to anyone about that. 'When you put down poison for the rats, how long does it take for them all to be gone?' I asked at last.

'They sicken within the day and usually die within two, though it depends a little on how strong they are and how much they've eaten,' he replied, giving me a very odd look indeed. 'I dunno why everyone's asking about poison. I 'ad that there Mr Hatton asking me if I had sold any or lost any yesterday.'

The Queen must have asked Mr Hatton to make some discreet enquiries.

'And have you?' I asked.

'No, I'm very careful with it,' he said, look-ing highly insulted. 'I don't even keep it at the palace. You think I want to end up hanged, drawn and quartered if the Queen should find my rat bait in her food?'

I decided I would have to send Masou back

tomorrow to see if the rat was sickening. Certainly the little furry animal seemed perfectly happy and healthy so far: no cramps, no vomitus and no flux – as far as one can tell with rats – which suggests that Sampson Childs may be innocent after all.

Oh, Lord, I must stop writing now, for I am late to attend upon the Queen.

About noon, within my chamber

First thing this morning Ellie came to collect the dirty laundry from our chamber and she brought a message from Masou. He had been back to see the rat-catcher and reported that the rat which had eaten the sweetmeat was still looking very hale and hearty and not the least bit sick! So there seems to be no doubt at all that the Turkey sweetmeats were quite innocent, which means that Sampson Childs is not a poisoner.

Of course I was pleased for the rat – and for the old player – but once again I found myself without a suspect. Since Mr Hatton's questions had proved it very unlikely that the poisoner was getting his arsenic from the rat-catcher, I decided to investigate the only other place where I knew arsenic could be found – the painters' workroom.

I had planned to ask Mrs Teerlinc whether any of her paint supplies had gone missing or whether – even if Sampson Childs was innocent – his yellow paint could be the source of the arsenic, but in the end I didn't need to, for I could hear her shouting from the bottom of the workroom stairs!

'By my faith!' she was shouting. 'This is beyond a jest.'

As I entered the room, I saw Nick Hilliard standing with the other limners, and they were all looking very hangdog.

'Only last month I had a large order come from the apothecary,' Mrs Teerlinc continued, 'viz ceruse white and red – orpiment, malachite, lapis lazuli and crimson. And now you tell me we are near the end of our stocks again! How is it possible, gentlemen? Certainly we paint a great deal, but not that much. Has any one of you a secret commission to paint the walls of your brother's dining chamber? Hmm? Or are you selling paint that the Queen has paid for?' She was scowling because she obviously thought that was exactly what was happening. 'Well?' she demanded.

Nobody said a word; they were all staring at their boots and the floor and the ceiling.

'By God, I shall have the locks changed upon the colour closet. I shall not have the Queen cheated in her own house!' Mrs Teerlinc declared.

I was so excited I could hardly breathe. Orpiment was missing! So it seemed that I had found out where the poisoner was getting his arsenic. I decided I must set a watch upon the workroom to see if any more paint is taken, and if so, by whom. I suspect that the thief is taking all kinds of paint to conceal the fact that he is after the poisonous orpiment. Of course, Mrs Teerlinc locks the whole place after sunset, so there need only be a watch during the less busy times of the day.

I was about to go when Mrs Teerlinc spotted me and came bustling over. 'Now, my dear,' she said. 'I have cancelled Lady Sarah's sitting for today because we have not sufficient paint. Did she not tell you?'

In truth I had forgotten there was to be a sitting. 'I'm sure she would have, but I haven't really seen her today,' I answered.

'And is the Queen's little dog any better?' enquired Mrs Teerlinc.

For a moment I couldn't think what she was talking about, and then I remembered my excuse for asking about orpiment poisoning. 'Oh, um, yes, he's much better. I must have been wrong about what he ate, for the rat-catcher is not allowed to put down poisoned bait while the Queen is in residence. Doubtless it was some bit of rubbish or an old sweetmeat he found.'

She smiled kindly at me. 'I am surprised you are here and not down there sighing over young Fitzgrey like most of the Queen's women,' she said, nodding at the windows that gave onto the Outer Courtyard.

I looked and it was like a flower garden for the bright kirtles of the ladies. And there were the players, trying to make a pyramid in the centre. 'No,' I told her. 'For my part I think he likes his own looks far too much to need anyone else's admiration.'

'Go to,' said Mrs Teerlinc, laughing. 'At least one young woman has sense.'

I had spotted Masou and Ellie down in the courtyard, so I thought I would join them. I curtsied and hurried down.

I sat down casually near the spot where Ellie was hanging about, gazing lovingly at Richard Fitzgrey and looking very like a calf with the bellyache. Masou was helping Will Somers instruct the players in the right way to build a pyramid of their own bodies, with the strong men along the bottom and then the boy players on top. For a wonder, they had it up, tottering slightly. And then Masou climbed his way to the top, where he stood carefully on the shoulders of the smallest boy actor.

At that exact moment Lady Sarah walked slowly across the courtyard, her shining red hair tumbling down her back. The pyramid wobbled as Richard Fitzgrey – who was supposed to be one of the strong men hold-ing it all up – tried to bow and wave at her. Everybody shouted at him, one of the boy actors panicked and jumped for it, and then the whole thing tumbled down and the players landed in a heap. Masou must have felt the problem beginning for he had jumped from the top, somersaulted in the air and landed neatly on his feet, laughing heartily. Nobody was hurt, except in their dignity, but everyone was very angry with Richard and shouted at him. He did seem a little embarrassed as he climbed to his feet again.

'Ooh, I hope he ain't hurt,' said Ellie.

'No, Masou's fine,' I reassured her.

She looked at me as if I were woodwild. 'I meant Richard,' she told me.

'Honestly, Ellie!' I said, quite cross with her. 'Richard may be nice to look at, but Masou's a *friend*.'

Ellie went pink and scowled at the ground. 'No harm in looking, is there?' she muttered.

I had to wait until Masou could leave off his tumbling lesson, because I shouldn't be seen talking to him really. I don't have any excuse to do so, whereas I can always claim I'm talking to Ellie about my linen.

At last Mr Somers said he could go, and then we all went casually in the direction of the copse. We headed under the archway and down through the garden behind the court-yard, though it was getting a little late. Masou was still laughing at Richard and making very rude jokes about why the pyramid had collapsed – far too rude for me to write here.

Ellie told me she'd offered to take a tray up to Carmina, and so got to talk to the cook who was in charge of her food. He was making a calf's-foot jelly specially to tempt her appetite.

'He's quite young, but he's very nice and he's cooked for the Queen herself!' Ellie said. 'She asked specially that he look after Carmina's food, you know, and he was very proud about it – 'e told me three times. He said the Queen had told 'im that since his great-grandfather cooked for *her* grandfather, and his grandfather and father cooked for good King Harry and young King Edward, she was right glad he was there to cook for her. And she knew he would be able to make something that would delight the maid who's sick.'

I smiled. The Queen is so clever! Somebody whose family has been cooking for the Crown so long would rather die than put anything bad in the food. I was glad she had made certain to protect Carmina. That confirmed that whatever is poisoning her, it isn't coming from the kitchens.

'Somebody has been stealing paint from the workroom,' I told Ellie and Masou.

'So what?' asked Masou.

I explained to him about yellow orpiment and how it is used to make arsenic. 'And I really need someone to keep a watch on the workroom,' I said, 'in case the poisoner comes and steals some more, before Mrs Teerlinc gets the lock to the colour closet changed.'

'I could climb the old oak tree in the orchard behind the Outer Courtyard – you can see the limners working from there,' said Masou thoughtfully. 'I know because one of the gentlemen was up there the other day watching Lady Sarah. He's lovesick for her, but she says she doesn't like him because he is too short.'

'You won't get in trouble for not teaching the players, will you?' I asked anxiously.

Masou shook his head. 'No, Mr Somers says if I can't keep a straight face when the players make a mistake, I should stay away. I don't know how he doesn't laugh, though; they are such fools – especially that Richard Fitzgrey.'

'He wouldn't dismiss you?' I asked.

Masou puffed out his chest and looked insulted. 'I am the best boy acrobat in his company,' he said proudly. 'He won't.'

So that was all arranged, and I left Masou to climb his tree and Ellie to go back to the laundry while I went to visit Carmina again.

She was very cross with me. 'You put nasty crumbs of charcoal all over my favourite sugared apricots and I had to throw them out!' she accused.

'Well . . . it was to strengthen your stomach,' I explained.

'I'm feeling much better, so I don't see why you're trying to poison me!' Carmina exclaimed.

That upset me so much that I nearly lost my temper and told her I thought someone *was* poisoning her, and it certainly wasn't me. But I managed not to because I didn't want to frighten her. She does seem better now — she has some colour in her face again and is less sleepy — so I promised I wouldn't do it again and went to my chamber.

And that is where I am now, busy scribbling in my daybooke, while Lady Sarah and Mary Shelton chatter on about — guess who?

– Richard Fitzgrey.

The Fifth Day of March, in the Year of Our Lord 1570

About midday

I am worried about Carmina again, for Mary Shelton has been to see her and says she has taken a turn for the worse this morning. Lots of Ladies-in-Waiting have visited, with custards and sweetmeats to tempt her to eat, but Carmina will eat next to nothing – which is a very good thing, in my opinion, because we cannot be sure what foods are safe. She is very pale and sweating, though there's still no fever. My Uncle Cavendish said he thought it could be a tertian fever, but Mary says that is nonsense because then there'd be a fever, wouldn't there? I must hurry and find the poisoner before it is too late. But how?

All this morning I had to attend the Queen while she received the French Ambassador in the Presence Chamber, which means standing behind her on the dais to attend to the train of her gown, and trying not to yawn while she talks in French and the Ambassador tries to answer her tactfully. The French are trying to persuade her to allow one of their princes of the blood to make suit for her hand in marriage, and so there's a great deal of flattery going on – you can tell from the Ambassador's tone of voice – which the Queen always enjoys greatly. Lady Sarah was there too, but she enjoyed it for she was pleased not to have to sit still in the workroom wearing hot, heavy robes. And I had no chance to write in my daybooke, of course – I had to wear the white damask with no apron and look very attentive and serious and not fall asleep.

At last the Queen gave me leave to go, and I came back to the bedchamber to change into my hunting kirtle ready to walk the dogs and—

Evening, in my bedchamber

I had to stop because Masou was knocking quietly on the door, looking very mysterious and excited. I was about to tell him off for risking coming to the Maids of Honour, their chamber – he has no good excuse, unlike Ellie, and if he were caught, a beating would be certain and they might dismiss even the best boy acrobat in the troupe – but he did not give me the chance.

'Come quick!' he said. 'I've been in the oak tree, watching the workroom for you all morning, and you'll never guess who I saw sneaking something into his belt pouch.'

I immediately left my chamber and hurried with him to the workroom. On the way we saw Ellie with a bundle of washing, and she had to come with us, of course.

'Who was it?' I asked as we hid behind one of the trees in the orchard behind the Outer Courtyard.

'That long-legged young limner Nick Hilliard,' said Masou triumphantly.

'No!' I exclaimed. I found it hard to believe he was the poisoner. He doesn't even know Carmina.

'It was,' insisted Masou. 'I saw him. While the thin lady was bringing old, blind Ned one of her tisanes and Mrs Teerlinc was busy with a tailor, Nick Hilliard took a lump of something, wrapped it in a bit of paper and put it in his pouch. I saw it clear as day.'

'Lord above,' I said, thinking hard. I knew Nick was short of money because of his love of card games and drinking. 'Mayhap the real poisoner is paying him,' I told Masou and Ellie. 'In any case, we must find out what he does with what he's got.'

'Here he comes!' hissed Ellie, who was keeping watch.

Nick Hilliard was whistling as he came through the back door of the workroom and headed along the side of the orchard towards the New Buildings. It was lucky we weren't at Whitehall because then he might have had lodgings in Westminster, or even in the City of London, which would have made it much more difficult to follow him, because it's always hard for me to leave the palace without the other Maids of Honour.

Nick hurried down a little alley and into an open square where some chickens were pecking about in the mud. We followed him cautiously, trying not to get so close that he'd notice us, but not wanting to risk losing track of him either. He took a winding path, twisting and turning through the New Buildings until he reached a low doorway and a staircase. We watched as he ran up the steps. We were stuck! If we tried to follow him upstairs he'd be sure to spot us, but we couldn't possibly see what he was up to from the ground. We looked around frantically for a handy tree, but there was none.

Then Masou spotted a balcony being repaired on the building opposite. We climbed up one of the ladders – of course, Masou had to show off by shinning up one of the scaffolding poles – and found we could see across to the room opposite quite clearly. It was a large room with big windows, and it was full of wood panels and pieces of canvas stretched on wooden frames. All of them were at different stages of completion.

We heard the door bang and had to duck down quickly as Nick entered the room and glanced out of a window.

'Ooer!' gasped Ellie suddenly.

I looked where she was pointing and saw Richard Fitzgrey striding along the alley, looking a little furtive.

We peeked over the poles of scaffolding, expecting him to go straight past. But to our surprise he went in through the same low doorway Nick Hilliard had used, and we heard his feet on the stairs.

Ellie looked at me in dismay. 'Oh, no,' she said. 'I can't believe that lovely Richard Fitzgrey is involved in a poisoning.'

I didn't know what to say to her. I was utterly confused. Whoever I had been expecting to buy the poisonous orpiment from Nick Hilliard, it had surely not been Richard Fitzgrey. My mind was racing as I tried to fathom what Richard could possibly have against poor Carmina. I could think of nothing. Perchance he was here in error, or mayhap Richard was selling the poison on, or perhaps he was here for some other reason entirely, I thought. It was certainly a puzzle, and we could do nothing but sit and wait and watch.

We heard the door open and voices, and we saw Richard enter Nick's room and sit down. But we couldn't see Nick properly through the windows. The men were talking but we couldn't hear their words clearly – it was terribly frustrating.

Richard sat there for a long time. Eventually, Ellie was worried about getting back to the laundry, Masou was anxious that Mr Somers would miss him and I was wondering if I would be in trouble with Mrs Champernowne. We had just decided to give up and climb down, when Richard stood up and a moment later we saw him coming back down the stairs. He emerged from the doorway and headed back towards the main part of Nonsuch Palace again.

'I must return to Mr Somers,' said Masou, looking extremely smug. 'But I told you it must be the posing players, and now here is the proof.' He swung himself down one of the poles and dropped to the ground.

'Masou!' I called, scrambling down a ladder in a hurry. 'Wait – I really need to talk to you.'

'Why?' he asked. 'We've found the poisoner. Obviously Richard Fitzgrey is paying Nick Hilliard to take poisonous paint from the work-room, so that he can use it to poison your friend. It's exactly what I would expect of a player.'

'That's manure,' said Ellie – well, she almost said that; I've changed it to make it more respectable.

'Ellie's right, Masou,' I put in. 'We can't know that's the case. We didn't see Nick hand over the poison. And why would Mr Fitzgrey want to poison anybody, leave alone a Maid of Honour he does not know at all?'

Masou shrugged. 'He's a player so he's half Bedlamite anyway,' he said. 'Maybe he thinks he's in a play; I expect he just thinks it would be entertaining—'

'Lady Grace!' interrupted a voice behind us. 'What on earth are you doing here?'

I spun round. There was Nick Hilliard standing in the entrance to the stairway, with his jerkin half on and hanging from one shoulder.

'Um, I . . .' I began nervously.

Masou and Ellie moved closer to me. I was actually quite scared. If Nick was stealing poison for Richard Fitzgrey, he wouldn't want me to tattle-tale about it; who knows what he might do? He could get violent, or maybe even kidnap me – though that would be dangerous in broad daylight, so close to the palace. And though Nick has long legs, I think Masou could certainly outrun him to raise the alarm. Still, it was quite scary.

However, I wasn't going to let Nick know I was afraid, so I took a step forward and pointed at him. 'We saw you stealing from the workroom!' I said loudly. 'What were you going to do with all the poison you took?'

For a moment I thought he might try and brazen it out, but then he looked down and sighed. 'I need paint,' he said quietly. 'I *must* have it. And I cannot afford to buy it – or not enough of it, anyway.'

I narrowed my eyes and stared at him suspiciously. Was it possible he was stealing poisonous paint . . . to paint with?

'Come and see,' he said. 'I'll show you what I'm doing with it.'

I hesitated. Ellie stepped forwards and I could see she'd quietly picked up a rock, which she was hiding in the folds of her old blue kirtle.

'What'll you do to m'lady if she comes into your lodgings with you?' she demanded rudely.

Nick stepped back a fraction and spread his hands. 'Nothing, I swear,' he replied. 'I just want to show her what I need the paint for.' There was a pause while Ellie glowered at him suspiciously. 'Look,' he said, 'the only thing I care about is my painting. I would not risk my position at Court for anything else.'

'Masou,' I said quietly, 'would you wait five minutes until we come down?'

Masou nodded, folded his arms and leaned against the wall, staring at Nick threateningly through narrowed eyes.

Nick turned and led the way up the stairs. Ellie and I followed. We went in through a small door at the top where Nick had to duck his head.

Inside, a straw pallet and some blankets lay on the paint-splattered wooden floor. The rest of the room was filled with canvases and panels, all half-finished, as we had seen from the scaffolding. There were some miniatures, painted on vellum backed with a playing card, and I saw one, nearly finished, of the Queen herself in the robes Sarah had been wearing in the workroom – he must have done it from memory.

In the centre of the room was an easel with a truly enormous canvas up on it. Brightly coloured warriors fought across the canvas, and a big wooden horse towered over everything.

'While I am working for Mrs Teerlinc at the workroom, I have no time to seek a patron,' he explained. 'And so I must . . . borrow for my art. See, this picture has a classical theme – the Sack of Troy!' He gestured proudly at the big canvas.

'So why was Richard Fitzgrey here?' I asked.

'He was modelling for me, in exchange for a miniature I am making of him,' Nick told me. 'I needed a well-looking man for the face of Paris. Look – here are a few chalk and graphite studies I have done of him.'

It was very odd – when I looked at the big canvas I could see that the figures and colours were very good, but somehow the picture didn't fit together properly. It looked rather jumbled. But the small studies of Richard Fitzgrey were marvellous – it was just as if he was looking out of the paper at us.

'What do you think?' Nick asked, with a funny, nervous expression on his face.

'Well . . .' I began slowly, not wanting to hurt his feelings.

'I think the limnings you've done of Mr Fitzgrey are beautiful,' breathed Ellie. 'I wish I could have one. They make him look even more handsome than he is already!'

'But the big painting? The classical theme, my lady?' Nick pressed.

'Well,' I said. 'It's just that, there's so much happening, and it's all a bit mixed up.'

'That's the Italian style!' he told me, sounding very annoyed.

'Hmph!' sniffed Ellie. 'I dunno why you want to go wasting your time making huge great canvases when you can draw a picture of someone what could be breathing it's so good.'

I couldn't have put it better myself. Nick blinked at her for a moment.

'I mean,' continued Ellie, waving a skinny arm at *The Sack of Troy*, 'who'd want that on their chamber wall? It'd give 'em nightmares for sure. But if I had any money – which I don't, mind – I'd give you all of it just for one of these here limnings of Richard to keep after 'e's gone away.' And she sighed a bit.

'But with my gift, I . . . I should be painting important subjects,' stammered Nick.

'Why?' demanded Ellie. 'And what's more important than people? I'd do anything to have a limning of myself as good as that one of Richard, so my children could know what I looked like when I was young.' And she wiped her nose on the back of her hand and crossed her arms.

Nick looked at me, confused. 'What do you think, Lady Grace?'

'I think Ellie's right,' I said frankly. 'Everybody wants a picture of their love – or their mother, father or child – for themselves and to show to their friends. If you can do these little paintings so beautifully, why not?'

Nick was staring at us thoughtfully, and I didn't really want to interrupt his musings, but I had to ask. 'You don't seem to be using a lot of yellow, so why did you steal more orpiment today?' I demanded.

He looked confused. 'But I didn't.'

'Yes, you did. Masou saw you sneak it into your belt pouch. That's why we followed you.'

Nick laughed. 'It wasn't orpiment I stole,' he said. 'I don't need orpiment yellow for what I'm painting. Look!'

And he felt in his belt pouch, pulled out a bit of paper and unscrewed it to reveal a lovely bright lump of . . .

Blue lapis lazuli.

'Oh!' I exclaimed, starting to feel very annoyed with Masou for bringing us on a wild goose chase. But then I hadn't told him what colour orpiment is, and when he saw Nick stealing, he must have assumed that he was taking orpiment.

'Lapis lazuli is terribly expensive,' Nick was saying. 'And I need a lot of it for the sky above Troy. I just can't afford to buy enough paint. Please don't tell Mrs Teerlinc. She might have me dismissed.'

'Hmm,' I murmured.

Ellie was wandering about the room, being careful not to step in the wet paint spots, and looking at the smaller studies Nick had done of other people from Court. There were some studies of the Queen – one of her laughing, which was very undignified and not like her usual portraits, but so real you could practically hear the roar of it.

'All right,' I said finally. 'But only if you promise not to steal any more paint. Couldn't you paint some more of those little portraits for a while, and sell them and get money that way?'

He smiled. 'Perhaps I could,' he said eagerly.

'Mrs Teerlinc thinks so. I will certainly think again about struggling to finish my masterpiece of Troy after your friend's comments.' He looked across at Ellie, who was gazing soulfully at the study of Richard again. 'You can have that,' he said, 'in thanks for your wise advice.'

Ellie turned to him with her eyes shining. 'Can I?' she breathed. 'Can I really? I never had anything so beautiful before.'

'You can,' he told her, and took down the piece of paper very carefully, pinned it to a small piece of wood, and then wrapped it around with another piece of paper to protect it.

Ellie put it reverently into her petticoat pocket and curtsied her thanks and then we clattered back down the stairs.

Masou sprinted away to his tumbling as soon as we'd told him everything. Ellie and I went a little more slowly back to the garden, before she disappeared to the laundry and I went to find the other Maids of Honour.

I found them all whispering outside Carmina's bedchamber; even Lady Jane was looking worried. There was an awful sound of somebody groaning and being sick within, and then we heard my Uncle Cavendish's voice. He was talking very softly to Mr Durdon.

'They're bleeding her some more,' said Mary Shelton. 'I don't think they know what to do – she's so much worse. She has terrible cramps in her belly.'

I bit my lip, because it reminded me of what Nick had said about the pains feeling as if a rat were clawing its way out of your belly. My eyes filled with tears. It will be so awful if I don't solve the mystery before I can save Carmina.

Just then Mrs Champernowne came out, looking weary and drawn. 'Poor child,' she said. 'Perhaps her mother will help her a little.'

'Have you sent for her?' I asked anxiously.

'Yes, my dear,' she said. 'The messenger left this morning and will be there by nightfall, since he is riding post. But her mother will likely not be here for another two days at the earliest, for she cannot ride like a young man.'

It is rather squashed in our bedchamber tonight, for the Queen ordered truckle beds to be brought in, and now we have Penelope and Lady Jane sleeping here with us, so that Carmina may have some peace and quiet. Mrs Champernowne will be with her overnight. For a wonder, everyone is so concerned about Carmina that Lady Jane and Lady Sarah are not even quarrelling!

'The Queen is worried she may have left it too late,' Mary Shelton has just whispered to me as I write.

Perhaps Her Majesty delayed to see what I could do. And I really thought I was on to the truth with Nick Hilliard's thieving, but it turned out to be nothing to do with the poisoning. I feel dreadful.

The Sixth Day of March, in the Year of Our Lord 1570

Before dawn

I've just woken up and it's still dark. I only have the watch candle to write by and I simply must make a note of what came to me while I slept. Nick said he didn't need the yellow you get from orpiment, but Mrs Teerlinc definitely said orpiment was missing. So somebody else must have taken it from the workroom. I just need to work out who. This puzzle is becoming more and more of a mystery. Every time I think I may be on to the poisoner, I seem to reach another dead end. I'm not giving up, but I know that I am running out of time – and so is Carmina.

Later upon the same day, in the Queen's Presence

Mrs Champernowne has just been really rude to me – and I don't think it is only because she was up all night looking after Carmina!

To begin at the beginning. I was attending the Queen at her toilette this morning and very, very carefully brushing her hair, when I overheard something interesting. Lady Helen was bringing the Queen her bread and beer, while Mrs Champernowne mixed the paints for Her Majesty's face. As Ladies-in-Waiting sometimes do, Lady Helen went on one knee to the Queen, and asked very prettily if there was to be a jousting contest soon. Her uncle is the Queen's Champion, and I happen to know her brother is considered very good at jousting. I expect her brother has laid out thousands of pounds on jousting armour and a charger, so he can impress the Queen.

But Her Majesty made a face and shook her head. 'Not soon, I am afraid,' she said. 'Since that terrible tragedy with the young Lord Harrington and Carmina's father, Piers Willoughby, I think it would not be tactful.'

Lady Helen sighed but said, 'Yes, Your Majesty,' and withdrew.

I was so shocked I stopped brushing for a moment. I had forgotten that Harrington was the name of the young man killed. I had a terrible cold when the joust happened, and besides, the name meant nothing to me at the time. But now I remembered that Harrington was the name of the family Carmina's family were at feud with, until the Lord Protector composed the quarrel. And I wondered if, perhaps, the feud could have been revived – in which case it could be that the Harringtons were behind the poisoning of Carmina! It made a lot of sense. Mayhap they did not believe that the jousting tragedy had been an accident and were now seeking revenge on the Willoughbys.

I realized I had to find out more about which

Harringtons might be at Court. But I didn't dare ask any of the other Maids, because I knew it would immediately start them gossiping. Besides, they might not even know. I needed to talk to someone who knew everything about everyone at Court.

I thought about it all through the Queen's toilette. In the end I decided there was nothing for it but to ask Mrs Champernowne, who knows pretty much everything about the people around the Queen, having served Her Majesty since she was only a girl herself.

So I made sure I was the one nearest to her when we all gathered in the Queen's Withdrawing Chamber. One of the other Ladies-in-Waiting was sitting with Carmina now, and although Mrs Champernowne was looking very tired, she wouldn't admit it. She asked me to help her by holding a skein of wool, so she could roll it up into a ball. It's a boring thing to do, but for once I was pleased, as it gave me a chance to talk to her

'Um, Carmina said something about the Harringtons when I was sitting with her the other day,' I began. 'Is that the same family as the young Lord Harrington who got killed in the jousting accident?' I asked it as innocently as I could, but even so, Mrs Champernowne gave me a very sharp look.

'Why, yes, it is,' she said, and sighed. 'John Harrington was the only son. The terrible thing was that even though the tragedy was pure accident, because Piers Willoughby survived and John did not, there was a lot of ill-favoured whispering about it. Some suggested that Willoughby had caused it deliberately, to be avenged on the Harringtons – there used to be a feud between the families, you see. Of course, Carmina's father would never have done that, for he is a most gentle, kindly soul, but people will gossip. And the boy's mother took it worst of all—' She broke off suddenly. 'And if you behave yourself, Lady Grace, and keep your new kirtle clean and unspotted, look you, I shall teach you to knit your own stockings as Mary Shelton does,' she finished, as if that was what we had been talking about all along.

I'm afraid I was so bored by the wool-winding I wasn't very quick this morning. 'Yes, but didn't the Harringtons . . . ?' I pressed.

But Mrs Champernowne frowned at me. 'Shhh!' she said, looking very significantly at Lady Horsley, who had just come in with Lady Seymour.

'Why?' I asked, forgetting I ought not question to the Mistress of the Maids. 'I just wanted to ask—'

'For Heaven's sake, Lady Grace!' scolded Mrs Champernowne. 'Can you never stop chattering and asking and gossiping?'

Well! I did stop talking but I think that is most unfair. I *don't* chatter, and I certainly *don't* gossip – or not half as much as everybody else at Court does, anyway.

After an age of more tedious wool-winding, Mrs Champernowne finally finished. I have made haste to write down all I have learned, but I must say I think Mrs Champernowne is a nasty old—

A little later, still in Her Majesty's presence

Lord above! That was close. And while Mrs Champernowne is sometimes very unreasonable, this time I have to admit she wasn't at fault. But I had to shut my daybooke quickly, and some of the ink has smudged badly so I can hardly read what I wrote – which might be as well, for Mrs Champernowne almost saw my words!

Well, not long after she had snapped at me, she actually apologized! I nearly fainted dead away on the spot, like Lady Jane at a spider or something. Lady Horsley was called to attend the Queen by fetching a flagon of wine for her. After she had left the room, Mrs Champernowne leaned forwards and said, 'I am sorry I had to scold you so sharply, Grace, but it would not do to be discussing her son's death in front of Lady Horsley.'

I was confused. 'But I thought you said his name was Harrington?'

'So it was, child,' Mrs Champernowne confirmed. 'Do you not remember that Lady Horsley was first wed to my Lord Harrington the elder, look you? And then, when her husband died and her son inherited the title, she married again to Lord Horsley.'

'Oh, my goodness!' I gasped. 'I didn't know.'

Mrs Champernowne patted my hand. 'It's a sad tale,' she said. 'But don't be upsetting yourself, my dear, for it is all past and gone now.'

Only it isn't, of course! My mind is racing along so fast I can hardly keep up. But I think I just *might* have solved the puzzle at last!

The young Lord Harrington was Lady Horsley's son, and Carmina's father caused his death. It was a tragic accident, of course, but what if Lady Horsley didn't believe that? What if she believed the nasty rumours that Piers Willoughby had killed her son in a revival of the old feud? That might give her a very good reason to want to hurt Carmina, perhaps even murder her!

I must stop now. I can't sit scribbling. If I am right and Lady Horsley is poisoning

Carmina, I must do something to stop her immediately!

Afternoon upon the same day, in my chamber

Who would have thought that anyone who seems so kind could be so evil? I was trying to think of how I could get permission to leave the Queen's presence and go to Carmina, but my mind kept racing along, finding more and more connections between Lady Horsley and the poisoning. She is marvellously skilled at making sweetmeats, of course, and Carmina has eaten almost nothing but sweetmeats since she first fell sick. The sugared apricots are her favourite, and Lady Horsley has brought her hundreds of those. How convenient that they are yellow, so the fragments of poisonous orpiment don't show up.

And I suddenly realized where she had been getting the poison, too! I have often seen her visiting old Ned in the painters' workroom. I thought she was being kind, but more likely she was using Ned to gain access to the poisonous paint. It would have been easy, for he would never see what she took.

Just as my thoughts were scrambling over themselves, like players trying to build a human pyramid, Lady Horsley herself knelt to the Queen and asked permission to visit Carmina. With more poisoned comfits no doubt! The Queen nodded and she hurried away.

I jumped to my feet. 'Oh, no!' I gasped.

Mrs Champernowne tutted at me and frowned, and the Queen looked up from a very long report.

'What is it, Lady Grace?' she asked severely.

'Um, er, please may I have Your Majesty's leave to go and visit Carmina right away?' I stammered.

'You can see her this afternoon,' replied the Queen. 'My Lady Horsley is with her now.'

I didn't want to burst out with all my suspicions in front of everyone, especially when the Queen had particularly asked me to be discreet. So I went on my knees and said, 'Oh, please, Your Majesty. It's *vitally* important I go right now, before, um . . .'

The Queen was going to tell me off for arguing, I could see it on the tip of her tongue. But then she looked at me again. 'Very well,' she said, putting the report back in the box, 'but we shall all go. I had meant to visit my dear Maid of Honour myself, but press of business has kept me from it. Now we shall all visit Carmina.'

It took a terribly long while to organize, because first Lady Sarah and Penelope were sent to fetch ingredients, so the Queen could make a nice posset for Carmina with her very own hands. Then one of the gentlemen had to go and fetch a chafing dish and some hot coals from the nearest kitchen. And then we all had to gather together and form a proper escort for Her Majesty. If I were the Queen it would drive me quite mad with impatience.

We went through the archway to the passage where the Maids of Honour's chambers are, and I was having terrible trouble not rushing ahead to see what was happening to Carmina.

When we finally arrived, it all looked quite peaceful. Lady Horsley was sitting quietly next to Carmina's bed, with a pretty enamelled bowl on the table next to her. The tawny damask bed curtains were part pulled back, and we could see that Carmina was sleeping. She looked awfully pale and ill and thin.

Lady Horsley stood and curtsied to the Queen, looking puzzled and even a little concerned. I noticed that she quietly draped a napkin over the enamel bowl of sweetmeats next to her. I felt sure that the sweetmeats within must be poisoned, but I couldn't just say so. It's a terrible thing to accuse anyone of poisoning. Why, if a wife should poison her husband, it's called petty treason and she might burn at the stake for it! I needed proof before I could tell the Queen what I suspected and I racked my brains to think of a way to get it.

'My Lady Horsley,' said the Queen, 'I have decided that I have been neglecting my dear Maid of Honour, and so we have all come to visit. I will make her a posset to help keep her strength up.'

That provoked a tremendous bustle as the gentleman brought up the chafing dish, filled with white-hot coals. Lady Horsley reached to move her enamelled bowl off the table, to make room for the chafing dish to stand there on its little legs, but somehow I got there first, and picked it up myself – being very helpful, of course.

I lifted the napkin for a peek and, as I suspected, it was full of sugared apricots. I wasn't sure but it seemed there were flecks of brighter yellow on them. That gave me an idea for how to get proof of the poisoning. I would ask Lady Horsley to eat one of her own sugared apricots. If my suspicions were correct, she would say no, of course.

Lady Helen put a nice new earthenware dish full of milk on the grill over the coals, and Mrs Champernowne carefully broke and separated two new eggs. The Queen snapped her fingers, and Penelope brought a jar of pounded sugar loaf and a dish of cinnamon and cardamom pods. The Queen carefully dropped the cinnamon and cardamom into the milk as it started to warm through, and Lady Sarah brought a clean, lace-trimmed apron to go over the Queen's gown. Mary Shelton gave the Queen a spoon, and she started stirring the milk so vigorously that the chafing dish wobbled slightly.

All the fuss and movement woke Carmina. She blinked and shifted and then struggled to sit up in alarm. 'Oh my goodness, Your Majesty!' she gasped faintly. 'I didn't know you were here.'

The Queen smiled, and stopped stirring to put her hand on Carmina's poor, thin arm. 'Now, my dear,' she said. 'I have come to visit you and see how you fare. I am going to make you a lovely egg-nog to help keep your strength up.'

All the ladies were watching the unstirred milk nervously, as it started rising up the sides of the bowl. Mrs Champernowne reached delicately behind the Queen to stir it quickly and move it to a cooler part of the grill. The Queen didn't notice.

'You are so kind, Your Majesty,' whispered Carmina. 'I'm sorry, but I can't curtsy.'

'Do not be silly,' said the Queen, smiling fondly and still ignoring the milk. 'I do not expect you to carry on with all that Court courtesy when you are ill. Now, then . . .' She turned back to the posset – so Mrs Champernowne had to snatch her hand away – and started stirring vigorously again.

'Let us see, I remember Queen Catherine used to . . . Ah, yes.'

The Queen dropped the egg yolks straight into the boiling milk and stirred. Unfortunately, it was too hot and the mixture started to curdle. She snapped her fingers at Mrs Champernowne, who brought up a flask, and Her Majesty poured in aqua vitae and stirred again. That made the curdling even worse, and the coals were too hot now, so we could all smell burning. For all the Queen's stirring, the whole custard had turned into a sort of boozy scrambled eggs!

Mrs Champernowne tried to rescue it by picking up the bowl with a cloth and pouring it into a silver cup held by Penelope.

The Queen looked at it and prodded it with

a spoon. 'Well, it looks a little thick,' she said doubtfully. 'Perhaps I should add more sugar?' The Queen has a very sweet tooth.

'No, it looks lovely,' said Carmina, being gallantly tactful. She took the cup and a silver spoon and started eating a little of the egg-nog. She even managed to swallow some and smile, which made the Queen smile back. I really don't know how Carmina could, because the Queen's posset was a curdled mess of eggs and aqua vitae and burned milk – and all the stirring had broken up the cardamom pods and cinnamon stick, which Her Majesty had forgotten to strain out, so there were black seeds and bits of cinnamon in it as well.

The Queen smiled proudly. She doesn't do very much cooking, of course, and nobody ever dares tell her the truth about what she makes, so I'm afraid this was quite normal.

Carmina struggled to drink some more and went even paler.

Well, I decided I had to do something – Carmina couldn't go on like this. I took the napkin off the enamelled bowl and held it out to Lady Horsley. 'Why don't you have one of these lovely apricots, my lady?' I said.

'No, thank you, child,' she replied. 'They're for Carmina.'

'But Carmina can't eat them all, and you wouldn't want them to go to waste,' I pressed. 'Carmina always says how delicious they are.'

I picked one out with the sweetmeat fork that was in the bowl, and held it out to Lady Horsley.

'I never eat my own sweetmeats,' said Lady Horsley coldly. 'I take my pleasure from seeing others enjoy them.'

'But really, since you've gone to so much trouble to make them, it's only fair that you should have at least one,' I insisted.

At that exact moment Carmina squawked and put her hand to her mouth. Lady Horsley pushed past me, grabbed the bowl the Queen had used to make the posset, and held it under Carmina's head so she could be sick.

And it was not an accident that as Lady Horsley pushed me out of the way, she banged my hand so that the enamel bowl went flying, and all the sugared apricots fell to the floor – except the one I had speared on the silver sweetmeat fork.

'I'm so sorry, Your Majesty!' gasped poor Carmina. 'I couldn't help it . . .'

You might have thought the Queen would be annoyed at this ungrateful treatment of her posset, but she wasn't. In fact she was looking very thoughtfully at me.

I, on the other hand, was absolutely furious with Lady Horsley's clever attempt to avoid eating the apricots, which I was now certain were poisoned. 'Lady Horsley, ma'am,' I demanded, 'why don't you want to eat your own sugared apricots? Are you afraid?'

'I don't know *what* you're talking about!' snapped Lady Horsley. 'Calm down and behave yourself, child.'

Amidst all the fuss, the Queen stood up and stared, gimlet-eyed, from me to Carmina, who had stopped vomiting. Then the Queen turned to Lady Horsley and stared narrowly at her, too.

At a sign from Mrs Champernowne, the

gentleman approached quietly, and took the bowl and the chafing dish away.

'Perhaps it would be better to dismiss all these girls so we can sit quietly with Carmina, Your Majesty,' suggested Lady Horsley, in that kind soft, voice of hers. 'I think some of them are becoming a little hysterical.'

'No,' said the Queen judiciously. 'I was rather hoping you would answer Lady Grace's question.'

Lady Horsley turned white and blinked at the Queen. 'I'm s-sorry, Your Majesty. What do you mean?' she stammered.

The Queen beckoned me to stand next to her. 'Give me the sweetmeat, Grace,' she ordered.

I curtsied and gave it to her, my heart sinking into my shoes. The Queen didn't believe me either. Maybe I was wrong. Maybe Lady Horsley was another false lead.

'Now, Lady Horsley,' said the Queen pleasantly. 'Shall I try your sweetmeat?'

Lady Horsley's face was now as white as Carmina's. She licked her lips nervously as she answered, 'Well, I . . . It might not be to Your Majesty's taste.'

'No, no,' said the Queen, smiling coolly. 'I love sugared apricots.' She actually opened her mouth and brought the sweetmeat fork towards it.

I nearly screamed. Attempting to poison the Queen is, of course, treason – you get hanged, drawn and quartered for that. Lady Horsley looked old and ill and her mouth worked as she stared in horror. Then something seemed to give way inside her.

She gulped convulsively and put out her hand. 'Please do not eat it, Your Majesty,' she whispered. 'It is . . . it is poisoned.'

Everyone gasped at that, even the gentleman who had brought the chafing dish. Lady Sarah uttered a little scream, but Mrs Champernowne gave her a reproving look and she settled down at once. Poor Carmina just stared at Lady Horsley in wonder, as if she couldn't quite believe what was happening, and I felt an overwhelming sense of relief that the truth was out at last.

'*Is* it?' said the Queen grimly, immediately giving the poisoned apricot on its fork to the gentleman. 'Tell us everything.'

'I . . . I took orpiment from the painters' and stainers' workroom,' Lady Horsley said quietly.

'How?' demanded the Queen.

Lady Horsley didn't seem able to speak.

'I think she was pretending to help poor, old, blind Ned by bringing him tisanes for his eyes, and he couldn't see what she was taking when Mrs Teerlinc was busy,' I explained. Everyone knew I had been spending time in the workroom, so I did not think that it would provoke too much comment that I had worked this out.

'Is that true?' asked the Queen.

Lady Horsley nodded once. 'And I ground it and put it on the apricots and gave them to the Willoughby girl.'

'Lady Horsley,' said the Queen in a terrible voice, 'tell me why in God's name you would do such an evil thing as to poison Carmina, a Maid who trusted you and had done you no harm?'

'Why should Piers Willoughby have a child when my son is dead?' hissed Lady Horsley, her face screwed up in sudden rage. 'Why should *he* get away with continuing the feud by killing my son and cunningly making it seem like an accident? Two can play at that game, and I will even the score myself so my poor son can rest in peace.'

Carmina was cowering back in the bed with her hand over her mouth and tears in her eyes. 'But I thought you were looking after me!' she gasped to Lady Horsley.

Lady Horsley ignored her. 'There must be return for evil; if a man strikes me, why, I must strike him back,' she hissed. 'The Willoughbys murdered my only child, and so—'

'But it was an *accident*,' wept Carmina.

'A likely story! A very well-planned and careful accident, methinks, since Piers Willoughby was all but unscathed and my son was dead!' shouted Lady Horsley.

'*Enough*, madam!' shouted the Queen right back – and my Lord, she can bellow when she wants. Lady Horsley flinched as if she had been struck. 'How dare you bully my Maid of Honour in mine own face! How *dare* you seek to murder her by secret poison with a cover of kindness! It is an outrage, by God!'

Now Lady Horsley was pale as death and staring at the Queen, who had her hands on her hips, fire in her eyes and the most terrifying expression on her face. Slowly Lady Horsley sank to her knees.

'But were you not even afraid of being discovered and burned at the stake?' whispered Mrs Champernowne in horror.

'I knew I would not be discovered, because God favours my cause as it is only justice,' said Lady Horsley, now in a very strange sing-song voice. 'And my dear son John told me all would go well. He appears to me and tells me to avenge him, so you see, I had to do it.' And she turned to the Queen and held onto the Queen's gown and said, with tears in her eyes, 'You do see it, Your Majesty. You do understand that I had to take revenge for my son when he told me to?'

There was complete silence, except for Carmina's crying. I was staring at Lady Horsley.

A moment ago I had felt triumphant and clever at having solved the mystery successfully and in the nick of time. Now I just felt sick, because it was clear that even though Lady Horsley seemed normal, she must be completely Bedlam mad. Would the Queen send her to Bedlam hospital? It's supposed to be a horrible place where they chain and beat the poor mad people whose families send them there.

The Queen stared thoughtfully, and then beckoned over the gentleman, who was still holding the fork with the poisoned apricot as if it were an adder. She took it from him and laid it on a clean dish.

'Mr Ormond,' she said. 'Escort my Lady Horsley to her own chamber and set a guard on the door. We shall consider what is to be done with her, since it seems her motherly grief for her dead son has utterly stripped her of reason. I am not sure she is sufficiently *compos mentis* to stand trial. It may be she must simply be confined; I do not know. And call Dr Cavendish so we may see to it that Carmina has the right treatment for poisoning.'

So Mr Ormond took Lady Horsley's arm to help her up and led her out. She seemed to be talking to someone invisible as she went, reassuring him that all would be well and that she would succeed in avenging him after all.

The Queen sat down next to Carmina and stroked her hand to calm her, while a Chamberer came and carefully swept up the sugared apricots from the floor to take them away as evidence.

Later, my Uncle Cavendish examined them, and he said there was so much orpiment on them that if Carmina had eaten even one, she would have been dead for sure!

Now my uncle knows what ails her, he can treat Carmina properly – though the treatment is very nasty for her. First she has to purge – to empty her stomach and bowel as quickly as possible – and then she has to drink wine with bezoar stone boiled up in it. Bezoar stone is very rare, and it's said to be the best cure there is for poison, but I've heard it comes from the stomach of sick goats, so I think it sounds absolutely disgusting. Once she has drunk the wine with the bezoar stone, Carmina has to eat charcoal biscuits to soak up any poison that might be left. And then, my uncle says, with any luck — and no more poisoned sweetmeats — Carmina should recover.

I know Lady Horsley has been terribly wicked, but I still can't help feeling sorry for her. I know how terrible it is to lose your mother and father, but it must be even worse to lose a child. And it's bad enough when ladies at Court lose babies — which happens to everyone, I think — but to lose a child once he has grown into a man . . . It makes tears come to my eyes just thinking about it. If one's mind wasn't very strong to begin with, I can see how one might well run Bedlam at it.

Eventide upon that day

As I was writing in my daybooke this afternoon, Mrs Champernowne came in to say that the Queen wanted to speak to me immediately, so

I hurried to her Privy Chamber. When I went in and knelt she was alone. She made me get up and sat me down on her own stool. 'Now, Grace,' she said, 'I am very pleased with your investigation, especially because you managed it so discreetly and with no mad escapades. You have done very well indeed, but I am afraid I have some bad news for you.'

'Oh, Your Majesty, is Carmina going to die?' I asked fearfully.

'No, no, Dr Cavendish tells me she is young and strong and did not eat too much poison. She should make a complete recovery provided she eats plenty of charcoal in the next few days, which she has promised to do. But Lady Horsley, I'm afraid . . .' She paused and shook her head.

'What happened?' I asked, with a sudden sick feeling in the pit of my stomach.

'Lady Horsley had some pure orpiment hidden in her room, and when she was alone there under guard, in a fit of madness, she ate all of it.'

'Oh, no!' I gasped. 'Poor lady.'

'Sadly, your uncle was too late to help her. But before she died, she managed to say that she was sorry for hurting Carmina.'

I put my hands over my mouth and tried not to cry.

The Queen put her arm around my shoulders. 'Now, Grace, I have told you this so you would not be upset by tittle-tattle. But you must not blame yourself at all. You prevented a terrible wrong by your alertness and quick thinking, and Lady Horsley committed self-murder while her mind was deranged. You, Dr Cavendish and I are the only ones who know what really happened. So as not to shame her family, we shall give out that she died of a stroke brought on by regret at what she had tried to do to Carmina – which is near enough true – and she will have a proper burial.'

I was glad of that, for it would be horrible for Lady Horsley's body to be buried at a crossroads with a stake through the heart – which is what you're supposed to do with a self-murderer, in case their ghost walks.

'Do you think she will go to Hell?' I asked the Queen.

'She must face God's judgement,' she replied thoughtfully. 'As we all must. But God is infinitely merciful and knows all hearts, so nobody can say. I only want you to understand that by your investigation you did a great good, and saved Carmina's life.'

I nodded. I am very glad that Carmina is saved, though it is sad that Lady Horsley is dead.

'Grace, you know the comedy play is tonight?' said the Queen. 'If you have no stomach to watch it, simply tell Mrs Champernowne you have a megrim and you are excused.'

So I came slowly back to our chamber. Everyone else is flurrying around, exclaiming about Lady Horsley while they get changed and ready to watch the players' last performance for us. Lady Sarah is putting on her make-up an inch thick, while I am just sitting and writing this. I think I will not go to the play.

Much later, near to midnight, in my bed

It was Carmina asked me to go with her to the comedy play, for she wanted something to cheer her up after having to take so much horrible medicine. I gave her the packet of Turkey sweetmeats from Sampson Childs – after I had brushed the bits of charcoal and fluff off the box, which came from it having been in my petticoat pocket. She said she had not the stomach for sweetmeats yet and wasn't sure she would ever eat them again – especially not apricots.

Mrs Champernowne helped her dress in a loose velvet English-style gown, and the Queen sent her own litter to carry Carmina down to the hall. I went with her to keep her company, and we had the best view of the players apart from the Queen. Everyone of the household who could be there was crowded into the back of the hall; I even caught sight of Ellie, in the corner, under one of the piled-up tables.

Then the trumpets sounded, the players leaped onto the stage and I do not think I have ever laughed so much in all my life. The play told a tale of twins getting confused for each other – only the two twins were played by Richard Fitzgrey, who is so tall, and one of the boy players, who normally plays women and so is quite short and small. The twins had many adventures trying to escape their wicked stepfather, who wanted to steal their magic jewel. They disguised themselves as all kinds of things such as Moors, Maids of Honour – a kirtle didn't suit Richard at all, though the boy player looked quite pretty – dogs, horses, beggars and Irishmen, as their stepfather chased after them.

At one point they made the human pyramid with their friends, in order to steal back the magic jewel from an upstairs balcony. The pyramid fell down again and again, in a different funny way each time! Once it was because a boy player, in a red wig and a dress, wiggled across the dais with his bodice full of cushions. That made all the Maids of Honour simply shriek with laughter, even Lady Sarah, who went quite pink but still laughed. Not even Lady Jane could carry on looking haughty when Masou came in, dressed as a hairy dog, and pretended to chase rats in and out of the legs of the men supporting the pyramid – making the whole thing fall down again. Finally, the wicked stepfather caught them and there was a big battle, but all ended happily.

Carmina soon forgot her sore stomach and was laughing along with everyone else. I'm sure it has done her good, because her face at last had a little colour in it and her eyes were sparkling. 'You know, Grace,' she said to me, leaning over the side of the litter in the break between the two acts, 'I have been thinking about Sampson Childs. He really was a very good clerk – look how neatly this letter was written.'

She showed it to me and it was indeed very tidy.

'I'll show it to my mother when she arrives the day after tomorrow, and perhaps she will talk to my father and they can find a place for Sampson.'

At the end the players danced a very wild Bergomask and sang a song of farewell, praising the Queen as the Goddess Artemis and Queen of the Fairies, and all of us as her attendant spirits. And then Masou stole the show again, by bouncing through the dance as the dog, while juggling little toy rats.

The Seventh Day of March, in the Year of Our Lord 1570

Just past noon, at a window seat

I am so pleased. The Queen ordered Mrs Teerlinc to come and see her with some designs for her new bedhead, which is to be very elaborate. I was in the Presence Chamber when Mrs Teerlinc arrived. It was strange to see her out of her workroom and looking so worried. Nick Hilliard was with her, also looking rather pale and anxious. Mrs Teerlinc knelt to the Queen at first, along with Nick, but Her Majesty told her to rise.

'I am appalled and shocked that anything from my workroom could have come near to harming Your Majesty's people,' said Mrs Teerlinc, shaking her head and sounding more Dutch than usual. 'I am come to ask your mercy for old Ned Steyner, who is utterly distraught that Lady Horsley stole orpiment from his easel and nearly poisoned a Maid of Honour with it.'

'Lord above, Mrs Teerlinc, I do not blame him in the least,' said the Queen. 'My Lady Grace has told me he is near to blind and had no idea what was happening. Lady Horsley was pretending kindness to him, just as she did to Carmina. She fooled us all, including me, so I can hardly be angry with Ned.'

Mrs Teerlinc glanced cautiously at me. 'Had you not heard of our problems with all the paints?'

'Why, no,' said the Queen, smiling at me. 'But then Lady Grace is discreet quite beyond her years.'

Mrs Teerlinc smiled too. 'So I see. Well, Your Majesty, I am completely reorganizing stocks of our paint ingredients, which shall be much better controlled than before. A great deal went missing, and has now been found again in the wrong cupboard, but in all the confusion we did not realize that the orpiment had been stolen; that is a thing that will not happen again.'

Nick Hilliard was looking modestly at the

ground, very relieved. I realized that he had expected me to tell the Queen about his thieving, and so must have confessed all to Mrs Teerlinc and replaced the paint. I guessed he had come to beg the Queen not to dismiss him.

'A very good idea,' said the Queen, being tactful.

'Mr Hilliard here has brought you a gift of his own making,' added Mrs Teerlinc, sounding much happier.

Nick brought out a little package wrapped in silk, held it out to the Queen, and then backed away when she had taken it.

Her Majesty unwrapped it greedily; she loves getting presents, no matter how many she may have received in the past. 'Why, how lovely!' she cried. 'Look here, Lady Grace, it is a most tiny portrait of me.'

I leaned forwards to look at it. The portrait was the size of an egg. It sat in an ebony frame, most wondrously carved. And it was superb. The Queen, to the life, looking out of the frame with such command it was as if she was truly there. Her jewels glinted, her pearls shone and her silken robes glimmered.

The Queen was silent for a while, gazing at the tiny painting. 'Who did the limning?' she asked. 'Forgive me, Levina, but it was not you, I think.'

Mrs Teerlinc smiled and shook her head. 'No, no, not me,' she confirmed. 'Mr Hilliard did it. He has been working on it in secret, but had not the confidence to show it to Your Majesty before now. He even has a way of mixing pounded gold with resin, laying it on the vellum and then polishing it with a ferret's tooth so that it gleams. At last I have persuaded him to make more portraits!'

I hid a smile – not you, Mrs Teerlinc, I thought, but skinny little Ellie who spoke her mind.

'Superb,' said the Queen quietly. 'Quite superb. And more honest than many, Mr Hilliard, for I can see you have kept that slight hook in my nose which I often miss in portraits of me. I will have a great deal of work for you, I think. And while we are about it, who carved this delicate frame?'

'That was Ned Steyner,' explained Nick Hilliard, still flushed with pleasure at the Queen's praise. 'He says that when he carves, it does not matter that he cannot see, for he feels it all anyway.'

'Then I shall order him to work upon my bedhead,' said the Queen. 'And this I shall wear upon my belt. In fact, I believe I shall appoint you our official Royal Miniaturist, Mr Hilliard, to be sure you can make as many as I desire.'

She beckoned me, and I came and found a thick silk lace and hung the portrait upon the Queen's jewelled belt, next to her fan. Nick looked quite dazed: if the Queen is wearing his work and has appointed him Miniaturist to the Crown, every single courtier in the place will be clamouring to have something painted by him, and he can charge what he likes. No more need to steal paint, I think. I grinned at him. He smiled back, looking bemusedly happy, and then he winked at me. As for old Ned, I think he will be much happier carving, for he will not need to squint at all.

There is good news of Penelope as well.

She had a letter arrive from her parents this day, and when she opened it she squealed with excitement. She is usually such a quiet little person, but at this, her face turned quite pink and her eyes were sparkling. At first she was talking so fast nobody could work out what she was saying, but then Mary gave her a cup of wine to calm her.

It is all to do with a distant cousin. She has known him since she was a child, because his lands border on her parents' estates. She likes him very much and has missed him greatly since he went to university and she came to Court. Her parents and his parents have been negotiating for years and at last it is all concluded. The contract is drawn up, her dowry and jointure are decided and she is to be wed as soon as possible! And because of her service to the Queen, Her Majesty has agreed for her marriage ceremony and feast to be held at Court – the which is a sign of great favour as the Queen normally hates for her Maids of Honour to be wed. Penelope's mother is quite undone with happiness about it. So now we all have a wedding to look forward to!

And Carmina is much better already. She didn't need the litter to get down to the Great Courtyard this noontide along with everyone else. Although we weren't really supposed to be there, practically every woman in the palace waved goodbye, as the players and their carts trundled out of the main gate between the hexagonal towers. Ellie was waving a kerchief. Masou was standing on a wall, wolf-whistling and shouting farewell.

As the last cart rumbled out, Richard jumped onto it, waved goodbye, and shouted that they would be playing at Merton, Farnham and all sorts of other places I've never heard of, all the way down to Cornwall – which is hundreds of miles away and only tin-miners, wreckers and pirates go there.

'And a last great thanks to our young friend Masou – the finest boy acrobat in the world,' shouted Richard, waving his hat at Masou, 'who taught me this!' And he stood on his hands on the back of the cart . . .

'Ooer,' said Ellie.

. . . until the cart went over a bump and Richard wobbled, kicked his legs and fell off.

'Told him he wouldn't be able to do it,' sang out Masou, still laughing and clapping as Richard rolled and bounced up onto his feet again 'You owe me a shilling, Mr Fitzgrey!'

And Richard took out his purse and threw a shilling to Masou, who caught it, looking delighted. Then Richard bowed extravagantly to all the girls and ran after the carts, shouting at them to let him back on.

'I suppose he's not so bad,' Masou admitted.

So now everything will calm down and *perhaps* the other Maids of Honour will start behaving sensibly. Meanwhile, I will stay on the alert for any crimes or mysteries that warrant investigation by the Queen's own Lady Pursuivant.

GLOSSARY

apothecary – an Elizabethan chemist

apple leather – a popular Elizabethan sweet-meat

aqua vitae – brandy

Barbary Corsairs – privateers or pirates from the Barbary States, authorized by their government to prey upon the ships of Christian countries

Bedlam – the major asylum for the insane in London during Elizabethan times – the name came from Bethlem Hospital

Bergomask – a rustic dance

Bey – a chief or a prince of the Ottoman Empire

bezoar stone – a hard, stone-like object from a goat's stomach, used by Elizabethans (unsuccessfully) to cure poisoning

bisket bread – chewy almond macaroons

blackwork – black embroidery on white linen

bodice – the top part of a woman's dress

bubo – an infected swelling, often in the armpit, associated with plague

bumroll – a sausage-shaped piece of padding

worn round the hips to make them look bigger

buttery – confusingly, this was a place where the barrels of beer, wine and brandy were kept for people to get drinks

cannonade – bombard with artillery

ceruse – a lead pigment used in painting

Chamberer – a servant of the Queen who cleaned her chamber for her – which the Maids of Honour and Ladies-in-Waiting, of course, could not be expected to do

chemise – a loose shirt-like undergarment

close-stool – a portable toilet comprising of a seat with a hole in it on top of a box with a chamber pot inside

comfit – a sugar-coated sweet containing a nut or seed

comfrey – a medicinal herb

consumption – a wasting disease such as tuberculosis

cramoisie – crimson cloth

cony-catcher – a cheat, often one who cheated at cards

coppice – a thicket or copse

Cordova leather – leather from the Spanish

city of Cordoba, which was famous for the high quality of its leatherwork

damask – a beautiful, self-patterned silk cloth woven in Flanders. It originally came from Damascus – hence the name

daybooke – a book in which you would record your sins each day so that you could pray about them. The idea of keeping a diary or journal grew out of this. Grace is using hers as a journal

demesne – lands, territory

distempered – disordered, deranged

doublet – a close-fitting padded jacket worn by men

dowry/jointure – money, goods and estates that a woman would bring to her husband on their marriage

farthingale – a bell- or barrel-shaped petticoat held out with hoops of whalebone

favour – a handkerchief or other token given to someone as a mark of the giver's favour

fleur-de-lys – a stylized way of drawing an iris – used in heraldry and fabric designs, etc.

garderobe – a private room

graphite – a soft form of carbon used in lead pencils

gumdragon – a vegetable gum used to make shaped sweets

henbane of Peru – also known as tobacco. In Elizabethan times it was regarded as a great cure for phlegm

humours – the fluids of the body which were thought to control health and temperament

journeyman – a skilled and reliable worker

kirtle – the skirt section of an Elizabethan dress

Lady-in-Waiting – one of the ladies who helped to look after the Queen and who kept her company

lapis lazuli – a semi-precious stone that is a rich blue colour

limn, limner – draw or paint; a painter

Lord Protector – Edward Seymour, Earl of Hertford. He was Edward VI's uncle and appointed by Henry VIII – in his will – to be 'Lord Protector of the Realm and Governor of the King's Person' until Edward was old enough to rule England himself *lye* – an ingredient in soap. It is strongly alkaline and was used for cleaning

Maid of Honour – a younger girl who helped to look after the Queen like a Lady-in-Waiting

malachite – a green mineral

manchet bread – white bread

marchpane – marzipan

marchpane subtlety – a sculpture made out of marzipan and then coloured

marmelada – a very thick jammy sweet often made from quinces

Mary Shelton – one of Queen Elizabeth's Maids of Honour (a Maid of Honour of this name really did exist, see below). Most Maids of Honour were not officially 'ladies' (like Lady Grace) but they had to be of born of gentry

masque – a masquerade, a masked ball

Master of the Revels – Court official in charge of entertainment for the Queen and her Court

megrim – a migraine headache

mummer/mumming – actor/acting

Mussulman – an old word for Muslim

New World – South and North America together

orpiment – arsenic trisulphide, usually orangey-yellow in colour. Used as a pigment for yellow paint in Elizabethan times

Painted Passage – a decorated passage of some sort was usual in the Queen's palaces so that the Queen could process down it and impress those subjects waiting to ask her for favours. Such a passage is mentioned in Court accounts simply as the 'painted passage'

partlet – a very fine embroidered false top, which covered just the shoulders and the upper chest

pasha – title given to a man of high rank in Turkey or North Africa

penner – a small leather case which would attach to a belt. It was used for holding quills, ink, knife and any other equipment needed for writing

plague – a virulent disease which killed thousands

posset – a hot drink made from sweetened and spiced milk curdled with ale or wine *post/riding post* – to travel very quickly by changing horses at different stages along the route, so that each horse is fresh and thus capable of greater speed

pounce – a way of transferring a design for embroidery. The design would be drawn on stiff paper and lots of little holes would be pricked with a needle along all the lines The paper would then be placed over the fabric to be embroidered, and powdered chalk or carbon would be sprinkled over it so that it fell through the holes, leaving an outline of the design on the fabric. The paper would then be removed and the embroiderer would tack along the lines made by the chalk to keep the design clear when the chalk rubbed off. Once all this had been done, the proper embroidery work could start

Presence Chamber – the room where Queen Elizabeth would receive people

pulses – the points on the body where the rhythmical beat of the heart can be felt

pursuivant – one who pursues someone else

Queen's Champion – combatant who rode and fought on the Queen's behalf

Queen's Guard – these were more commonly known as the Gentlemen Pensioners – young noblemen who guarded the Queen from physical attacks

raiment – clothing

samite – a rich silk fabric interwoven with gold or silver

Secretary Cecil – William Cecil, an administrator for the Queen (was later made Lord Burghley)

silk woman – serving woman in charge of caring for fine silk garments

small beer – weak beer

stainer – one who stained a wooden panel or canvas with colour

stays – the boned laced bodice worn around the body under the clothes. Victorians called it a corset

stomacher – a heavily embroidered or jewelled piece for the centre front of a bodice

sweetmeats – sweets

tabaca – tobacco

ten-day-old urine – ten-day-old urine was used in the laundry for removing stubborn stains!

tiring woman – a woman who helped a lady to dress

tisane – a medicinal hot drink made from herbs

truckle bed – a small bed on wheels stored under the main bed

tumbler – acrobat

vein/open a vein – a cut made in a vein to let out 'bad' blood. This was used as a cure for almost anything!

vellum – fine parchment made from animal skin

veney – a bout or round of sword-fighting

vomitus – sick

wand of office – a white rod, about two foot long, which was a Court official's badge of office

watch candle – a night-light

Withdrawing Chamber – the Queen's private rooms

withies – thin, flexible twigs and branches

woodwild – crazy, mad

THE FACT BEHIND THE FICTION

In 1485 Queen Elizabeth I's grandfather, Henry Tudor, won the battle of Bosworth Field against Richard III and took the throne of England. He was known as Henry VII. He had two sons, Arthur and Henry. Arthur died while still a boy, so when Henry VII died in 1509, Elizabeth's father came to the throne and England got an eighth king called Henry – the notorious one who had six wives.

Wife number one – Catherine of Aragon – gave Henry one daughter called Mary (who was brought up as a Catholic), but no living sons. To Henry VIII this was a disaster, because nobody believed a queen could ever govern England. He needed a male heir.

Henry wanted to divorce Catherine so he could marry his pregnant mistress, Anne Boleyn. The Pope, the head of the Catholic Church, wouldn't allow him to annul his marriage, so Henry broke with the Catholic Church and set up the Protestant Church of England – or the Episcopal Church, as it's known in the USA.

Wife number two – Anne Boleyn – gave Henry another daughter, Elizabeth (who was brought up as a Protestant). When Anne then miscarried a baby boy, Henry decided he'd better get somebody new, so he accused Anne of infidelity and had her executed.

Wife number three – Jane Seymour – gave Henry a son called Edward, and died of childbed fever a couple of weeks later.

Wife number four – Anne of Cleves – had no children. It was a diplomatic marriage and Henry didn't fancy her, so she agreed to a divorce (wouldn't you?).

Wife number five – Catherine Howard – had no children either. Like Anne Boleyn, she was accused of infidelity and executed.

Wife number six – Catherine Parr – also had no children. She did manage to outlive Henry, though, but only by the skin of her teeth. Nice guy, eh?

Henry VIII died in 1547, and in accordance with the rules of primogeniture (whereby the first-born son inherits from his father), the person who succeeded him was the boy Edward. He became Edward VI. He was strongly Protestant, but died young in 1553.

Next came Catherine of Aragon's daughter, Mary, who became Mary I, known as Bloody Mary. She was strongly Catholic, married Philip II of Spain in a diplomatic match, but died childless five years later. She also burned a lot of Protestants for the good of their souls.

Finally, in 1558, Elizabeth came to the throne. She reigned until her death in 1603. She played the marriage game — that is, she kept a lot of important and influential men hanging on in hopes of marrying her — for a long time. At one time it looked as if she would marry her favourite, Robert Dudley, Earl of Leicester. She didn't though, and I think she probably never intended to get married — would you, if you'd had a dad like hers? So she never had any children.

She was an extraordinary and brilliant woman, and during her reign, England first started to become important as a world power. Sir Francis Drake sailed round the world — raiding the Spanish colonies of South America for loot as he went. And one of Elizabeth's favourite courtiers, Sir Walter Raleigh, tried to plant the first English colony in North America – at the site of Roanoke in 1585. It failed, but the idea stuck.

The Spanish King Philip II tried to conquer England in 1588. He sent a huge fleet of 150 ships, known as the Invincible Armada, to do it. It failed miserably – defeated by Drake at the head of the English fleet – and most of the ships were wrecked trying to sail home. There were many other great Elizabethans, too – including William Shakespeare and Christopher Marlowe.

After her death, Elizabeth was succeeded by James VI of Scotland, who became James I of England and Scotland. He was almost the last eligible person available! He was the son of Mary Queen of Scots, who was Elizabeth's cousin, via Henry VIII's sister.

His son was Charles I – the King who was beheaded after losing the English Civil War.

The stories about Lady Grace Cavendish are set in the years 1569 and 1570, when Elizabeth was thirty-six and still playing the marriage game for all she was worth. The Ladies-in-Waiting and Maids of Honour at her Court weren't servants – they were companions and friends, supplied from upper-class families. Not all of them were officially 'ladies' – only those with titled husbands or fathers; in fact, many of them were unmarried younger daughters sent to Court to find themselves a nice rich lord to marry.

All the Lady Grace Mysteries are invented, but some of the characters in the stories are real people – Queen Elizabeth herself, of course, and Mrs Champernowne and Mary Shelton as well. There never was a Lady Grace Cavendish (as far as we know!) – but there were plenty of girls like her at Elizabeth's Court. The real Mary Shelton foolishly made fun of the Queen herself on one occasion – and got slapped in the face by Elizabeth for her trouble! But most of the time, the Queen seems to have been protective and kind to her Maids of Honour. She was very strict about boyfriends, though. There was one simple rule for boyfriends in those days: you couldn't have one. No boyfriends at all. You would get married to a person your parents chose for you and that was that. Of course, the girls often had other ideas!

Later on in her reign, the Queen had a full-scale secret service run by her great spymaster, Sir Francis Walsingham. His men, who hunted down priests and assassins, were called 'pursuivants'. There are also tantalizing hints that Elizabeth may have had her own personal sources of information – she certainly was very well informed, even when her counsellors tried to keep her in the dark. And who knows whom she might have recruited to find things out for her? There may even have been a Lady Grace Cavendish, after all!

A note on feuds

A feud is what happens when two entire families are embroiled in a private war with each other. The most famous feud is the fictional one between the Montagues and the Capulets in Shakespeare's play, *Romeo and Juliet*.

Feuding happens whenever law and order breaks down and people start taking revenge into their own hands, and acting outside the law. People did conduct feuds in Elizabethan England, but generally only in places a long way from the main centres of government and civilization – such as Cornwall, Wales and, most particularly, along the Anglo-Scottish border – because the government would put a firm stop to feuding whenever and wherever it could.

Very often the reasons for the feud were lost in the mists of time (he was rude to my great-great-grandma; they stole our sheep 200 years ago, etc.). But the hatred, and sometimes the killing went on, fuelled by whatever had been the most recent outrage.

During the Wars of the Roses (or the 'Troubles of King Henry VI's reign', as they were known in the fifteenth and sixteenth centuries) there were many aristocratic feuds. After Henry VII (Elizabeth's grandfather) took the throne, he spent the next twenty years crushing uppity nobles and sorting out the problems. But feuds could carry on simmering under the peaceful surface, and often did. There were also tremendous rivalries at Court, over who gained the King or Queen's favour or was granted a particular office; these could become very complicated and sometimes threatened to erupt into feuds.

Nicholas Hilliard

Nick Hilliard, who features in our story, was a real person. He was born in 1547 and trained as a goldsmith. In 1570 Queen Elizabeth I really did appoint him Court Miniaturist. He was particularly famous for his beautifully detailed, jewel-like miniatures, but he also painted larger portraits. As well as Queen Elizabeth, he painted other famous people of the time, including Sir Francis Drake and Sir Walter Raleigh. You can see a collection of his miniatures in the Victoria and Albert Museum in London.

Although Hilliard was an extremely success-ful painter, he had many financial difficulties and was actually imprisoned, briefly, for debt in 1617 (two years before his death in 1619). So perhaps the real Nicholas Hilliard wasn't so very different from the Nick Hilliard of our tale!

Levina Teerlinc

Levina Teerlinc was also a real person. Nobody knows exactly when she was born, but it is thought to have been around 1510, so she was quite old by the time Grace knew her. In 1545 she came from her home in Bruges to work for Henry VIII. Later she worked for his daughter, Elizabeth I. Like Elizabeth she was remarkable for achieving success in a career that had traditionally been the province only of men. Unfortunately, no paintings have survived which can definitely be attributed to Levina Teerlinc. She died in 1576.

Nonsuch Palace

We chose to set our story at Nonsuch Palace since it provides an interesting and lavish backdrop to this mystery. However, despite being built by Elizabeth's father, King Henry VIII, Nonsuch was sold after his death and did not come into Queen Elizabeth I's possession until 1592.

THE LADY GRACE MYSTERIES
ASSASSIN

By Grace Cavendish

MURDER AT COURT!

One suitor dead and another under
suspicion – and Lady Grace didn't even
want to get married! Can Grace, Queen
Elizabeth's favourite Maid of Honour, solve
the mystery and bring peace back to the
Queen's Court?

Open up the daybooke of Lady Grace
for a tale of daggers, death and a very
daring girl . . .

DOUBLEDAY
0 385 60644 3

THE LADY GRACE MYSTERIES
BETRAYAL

By Grace Cavendish

MYSTERY AT SEA!

Life as a stowaway on board an Elizabethan galleon — it's no place for a lady! But when her fellow Maid of Honour disappears with a dashing sea captain, Lady Grace knows she just has to investigate.

Hide away with the daybooke of Lady Grace, Queen Elizabeth's favourite Maid of Honour, for a tale of high waves and high adventure.

DOUBLEDAY
0 385 60645 1

THE LADY GRACE MYSTERIES
CONSPIRACY

By Grace Cavendish

SUSPICION AND BLOODSHED!

The Royal Court is on its summer travels and Lady Grace is sure something strange is going on. As Queen Elizabeth narrowly escapes a series of mysterious accidents, Grace must investigate just who might be behind the conspiracy. Could it really be one of the Queen's faithful friends – or even her latest suitor?

Delve into the daybooke of Lady Grace, Queen Elizabeth's favourite Maid of Honour, to discover a deadly dangerous plot . . .

DOUBLEDAY
0 385 60646 X